In the Mind's Eye

To Odile,
with my best wishes!
Barbara

In the Mind's Eye

Barbara Ponomareff

QUATTRO BOOKS

The publication of *In the Mind's Eye* has been generously supported by the Canada Council for the Arts and the Ontario Arts Council.

 Canada Council
for the Arts
Conseil des Arts
du Canada
 ONTARIO ARTS COUNCIL
CONSEIL DES ARTS DE L'ONTARIO

Cover design: Diane Mascherin
Cover art: Barbara Ponomareff
Author's photo: Constantin V. Ponomareff
Typography: Grey Wolf Typography
Editor: Luciano Iacobelli

Library and Archives Canada Cataloguing in Publication

Ponomareff, Barbara
    In the mind's eye / Barbara Ponomareff.

Issued also in electronic format.
ISBN 978-1-926802-49-7

    I. Title.

PS8581.O48I6 2011   C813'.6   C2011-903984-2

Published by Quattro Books Inc.
89 Pinewood Avenue
Toronto, Ontario, M6C 2V2
www.quattrobooks.ca

Printed in Canada

For Marc

"We do not know our own souls, let alone the souls of others. Human beings do not go hand in hand the whole stretch of the way. There is a virgin forest in each; a snowfield where even the print of birds' feet is unknown."

—Virginia Woolf

STRANGE, HOW HARD IT was for Caitlin to believe in the light when nighttime hung like a dense curtain just outside the streetcar window. Although on her way to work, she had not shaken off the aftereffects of yet another dream, more a nightmare really in its insistent return to the past. Beyond the window no trace of the day to come. Nothing but a sullen black which kept the world outside out of focus. Caitlin's face, as reflected in the window of the streetcar, appeared no more than a patch of ill-defined light.

Outside, hardly anyone was about. She could not help focusing on the dispiriting silt left on the road by winter's slow retreat. There in the dirty, frozen rims of snow all kinds of rubbish had become trapped; a derelict look that was echoed in the unending procession of smudged doors and grimy store windows. Everything she noticed seemed designed to reinforce a feeling of stagnation, even repugnance. As she got closer to her destination, the first streaks of daylight lit up the horizon and the blur of the small shops on either side of the street gave way to more familiar landmarks, the Trinity College grounds, the library. She would be there soon. Stepping off the streetcar, she lowered her face against the bitter March wind and crossed the road.

The very size of the building still jolted her, intrigued her. What had the architects been thinking of in designing a building of such gigantic dimensions? Its seemingly endless façade of light brick was ornamented at either end with graceful rotundas and topped by a reassuring cupola. It seemed to belie its true purpose, to house and treat the insane. Only the solid brick walls, on the average sixteen feet high, with their confining geometry, created a sharp division from the rest of the world and made one pause and hesitate to enter the spacious grounds inside. At this point in time, 1919, the Hospital for the Insane, Toronto, housed 1,269 patients as she had been told, and if not exactly welcoming, it seemed to have a sense of its own dignity and purpose.

Inside, greetings of "Good morning, Dr. Winstrum" met her on all sides. Being the first female staff member conveyed instant recognition and instant notoriety that she hoped would subside in due course. At this point the novelty of her being here was such that she felt her every move observed intensely; by the senior staff members, the nursing staff, and those patients who were well enough to take in that this young woman was one of their doctors. On the whole, she tried to ignore the small stir she caused, focusing instead on her professional purpose, which she hoped would lend her the necessary *gravitas* to make up for her youth and her sex.

As she hung up her heavy winter coat, heavier yet for being damp, she became conscious of the unnatural, almost thick silence of the room. Some parts of the building seemed to have a way of swallowing up daily existence and leaving instead a sense of life stilled – of time arrested – while others seemed to vibrate with tensions she could not as yet name.

Her immediate supervisor, Dr. MacLean, had obviously remembered to leave the files he had promised her on the desk. "Mainly numbers, statistics," he had said wryly, "but a way to start, to get to know what to expect here. Guidelines and some treatment protocols, to give you a sense of how we like to do things – come and talk to me about anything that does not make sense," and with that he had been off on his rounds. Friendly, helpful, paternal.

Hours later, she met him briefly in the hall, long enough to remind him that he was also going to assign her a few patients of her own, "to get your feet wet," as he had put it so quaintly. "Concentrate on the dementia praecox cases, the schizophrenics as we are learning to call them. Get a feel for them. Lots to choose from," he had chuckled. "Take your pick and make an in-depth study of two or three of them. Matron can help you with arranging the times. I recommend that you keep detailed notes – with a bit of luck we can find some time every Friday morning to review them."

In this way, a routine was taking shape that would grip her from the moment she entered the door until she left at the end of the day. Often, as she walked to the streetcar on her way home, she experienced a profound sense of displacement, as if having heard the heavy door of the asylum fall shut behind her, she was poised for a moment on the threshold between two conflicting realities. This short walk to the corner streetcar stop had become a necessary transition.

Coming home meant coming home to Mrs. Harris and her parents' house on Crescent Lane. Each time she turned the corner, she enjoyed the familiar sight of houses set well back from the road and from each other. Following the curve of the Rosedale Ravine, the crescent had a natural flow that made one forget the obsessive, rational grid of the city's streets elsewhere. Her parents had chosen well when they built this solid red brick structure with its bay windows facing south and southwest, its spacious verandah off the master bedroom and additional small balconies, more decorative than practical. As she closed the front door, the lead glass panes shivered slightly, fracturing the world outside.

Inside, as always, time seemed arrested. Mrs. Harris's sense of order allowed for no surprises. Caitlin's mail and the daily *Globe* would lie on the small table in the hall, her tea would be ready in the drawing room, Mrs. Harris would pour it, giving her a brief account of the day's lack of events, and dinner, as usual, would be at six-thirty sharp. It struck her suddenly that what she considered her routine, her life, was in effect a faithful copy of her parents' routine when she had been very young, except this time it was not her father unlocking the front door, picking up his mail, having his tea, but she herself, and there was no other person to share her day with.

Hours later, a dream captured her on a sandy beach: she was a child, her hair fell down loosely over her bare shoulders – it was summer. She was holding a shovel and was surrounded by sandcastles, as far as the eye could see. While she was patting and shaping the damp sand someone was calling her. She jumped up; her bare legs were dusted with sand as she ran with long strides up the hill towards a woman sitting in a deck chair. The woman was dressed all in white; her face was partly shaded by a parasol. Caitlin noticed how leaves traced shadows on her skin as she let herself fall into her lap. When she embraced her, she felt the cool cotton of her blouse next to her face. Tears streamed down her cheeks as she sobbed "Mama," only to wake up, abandoned once more.

The next day, a transparent sky seemed to promise a change of weather. It quickened her step. Matron had finally decided to remember her request for suitable candidates and gave her brief sketches of their condensed histories, various qualities and inaccessible minds, before returning sharply to her duties.

Philip Langley caught Caitlin's interest from the first because of his cool indifference, his raven-like stance. Dressed almost too formally in black, he kept his sleek dark hair longer than was usual. It tended to fall over his face, partially covering up his features as if to protect him. She found him standing tall and slim by a window where the sunlight slanted him indifferently, offering up different parts of him.

Matron had nodded agreement at her choice and walked up to him: "Philip, this is Dr. Winstrum, she is new to our staff and she would like to talk to you." As Caitlin had tried to catch his eye prior to stretching out her hand, she met nothing in return, only deeply serious brown eyes that swept her face briefly, emotionless to the core. She made a half-hearted attempt at small talk and then simply said that she would like to meet with him after lunch every other day. Matron would get him and show him the way to her office. She could hear her voice sounding too bright in contrast to the cloak of silence in which he had wrapped himself.

That is how they started. His file was meager, it gave just the bare facts: twenty-seven years old, admitted a year ago with a severe psychotic break following his premature discharge from the army where he had been deployed as a war photographer. Periods of florid intensity and illusions of grandeur had been followed by periods of relative lucidity or resolute silence. Restraining, and lately, hydrotherapy, had been used as "necessary." In contrast to the other patients who seemed for the most part eager to work on the grounds of the asylum farm in keeping with superintendent Workman's original vision, Philip preferred to stay inside, standing for much of the time by a window. His family, it appeared, was well off; they were paying for his keep and seemed to feel that that was the extent of their duty to him. This meant that Philip stayed in the more luxurious ward for paying patients, received better food and was not "made" to work. During those times when he felt better, he had shown himself to be a "well-read but caustic observer of asylum life," as his record insisted. Caitlin pinned her hopes on this last sentence and on her intuitive response to his haunting presence.

The first interview had been daunting. He had walked in, seated himself compliantly in front of her and let her talk. She had intended to be brief and encouraging, yet found herself chattering instead. Finally, she was able to stop herself and let his silence speak, while she listened to the metronomic sound of the ticking clock and the faint background of voices from down the hall. Eventually, she had felt his stillness seep into her own body. She tried to stay with it for as long as possible before saying somewhat too hopefully, too brightly, "Thank you, Philip, I will see you on Wednesday."

The next time she was prepared. She asked him straightforward questions about the place where he came from, the school he had attended and what he enjoyed doing. Factual questions which stayed away from anything that might be too personal, too threatening. Here and there she was rewarded with an answer, presented in a monosyllabic fashion, a toneless voice. At the end of their session she held a simple collection of facts in her mind – something, but not much. Philip seemed to leave as indifferent as he had come.

Several sessions later their meetings had become a challenge, a test of her faith in herself. Philip managed to pair silence with indifference and gave her the feeling that she did not really exist as a person who needed to be acknowledged. The occasional cryptic comment, just long enough to spark her interest, remained just that; he would not elaborate. Again, she felt that her own eagerness shut off his inclination to speak. There was no escaping the growing awareness of her ineptitude and inexperience.

Riding home on the streetcar that night, she resolved to learn the secret of meeting silence with silence, of learning to wait. After all, she knew something about that herself.

¤

Another session. Closing his eyes, Philip had dropped heavily into the chair in front of her. Had he found another way of negating her presence? The usual silence gathered and gelled between them and came close to suffocating her. Finally she broke it by saying, "Tell me about your life." He snapped back impatiently, "What life?" "*Your* life..." she said gently.

Surprisingly, he started to talk. As he did, she found herself floundering, felt her mind spring out of gear, her usual set of assumptions useless. What had happened to cause and effect, to specifics, to transitions? As he said at one point, "My words have no meaning anyway – so how can I tell you anything?" She had to tell herself to give herself time to understand *his* language, *his* thinking and perhaps, allow herself *not* to understand.

When their time was up, or more accurately, when he rose abruptly deciding he was finished, she felt drained. She saw him to the door before falling back into her chair thinking, "What am I supposed to do here? How am I supposed to help?" Her notes, when she was ready to face them, did not describe what he had said. Logic and words failed to reconstruct his broken narrative. Instead her notes were all about what she had felt while listening to him.

Dr. MacLean, when he had first outlined how she might approach her patients, had suggested that she might wish to see her chosen subjects more frequently, perhaps even daily. He had encouraged her to go beyond the cursory case notes to taking detailed notes of each session. Verbatim would have been ideal, but he realized that was not feasible. He suggested that she should try and enter each patient's world and move from empathy to genuine communication and understanding. Furthermore, he wanted her to combine her own notes with the clinical records kept by the nursing attendants. The staff had been trained to take down the number of hours slept, how much food was ingested, as well as any behavioral and mood changes for each patient under their care. He sparked her curiosity by stressing how little was known about schizophrenia itself, how Bleuler in Switzerland had only recently teased it out of the shadowy concept of dementia praecox. He also mentioned that he recently came across an article on the new "talking cure," which apparently could make a difference. Why not explore it? He would pass on some pertinent articles to her. After all, there was no dearth of subjects here. "We have a captive audience and controlled conditions," he had joked in his typically off-hand manner.

So here she was, armed with some textbook knowledge, very little life experience and not much else. She was feeling overwhelmed and bereft of clinical detachment. All in all, a humbling experience.

"May 7, 1919," she found herself writing in her clinical notes. Four years ago today, Nettie had died. She still saw the brutal headline in front of her – "1,224 lives lost," victims of what some papers had described as "wholesale murder, *not* an act of war." She thought wryly that today, after years of war, it would be hard to make a distinction like that.

In fact, she had only learned about the disaster the day after it happened. The seemingly impregnable Cunard liner, the *Lusitania*, had been torpedoed by a German submarine off the coast of Ireland. Initially, there had been cautious optimism about the number of survivors, yet as additional news became available, the death count kept rising. In the end, almost one hundred Torontonians were listed as dead. Nettie, her Aunt Antoinetta, and her new husband Thomas among them.

Nettie had been the closest approximation to a parent that fate had left her. After her parents' death, Aunt Nettie, only fourteen years older than she, had risen to the challenge, had moved in with her and become her parent and the mistress of the house. In the process the two of them had formed a close alliance. A mixture of maternal concern, sisterly affection and a favourite aunt's indulgence had characterized their bond. Best of all, Aunt Nettie had the same sense of humour and lively intelligence, that "glint" in the eye, that she remembered from her father. People's initial concern about the suitability of the two of them managing by themselves (with Mrs. Harris's capable collusion of course), had given way to respect for Nettie. Caitlin was clearly in good hands, and Nettie so obviously devoted to her, that everyone accepted their arrangement as probably the best solution to a terrible dilemma.

There had been times in the past when Caitlin felt pangs of guilt thinking that Nettie might not have begun a life of her own because of taking care of her. But Nettie would always laugh this off with "Have you ever thought that having you may have given me a perfectly good reason to stay away from marriage? If I ever meet the right man, Caitlin, you will hear about it!" she had finally promised her.

As Caitlin had become more and more absorbed in her studies and her own friends, she had often wished for someone to appear to rescue Aunt Nettie from spinsterhood. Yet when he did appear, she did not recognize him, although happily, Nettie did. Thomas Wellesley had been a university friend of her father's, a lawyer who, it was said, wrote poetry. After his wife died, Nettie had started to invite him over for Sunday dinners. When they had announced their engagement and married shortly after, Caitlin thought to herself, "And I am supposed to be observant..." Yet she was delighted for Nettie; Thomas seemed just right for her, he provided the calm surface that allowed Nettie's liveliness to sparkle to its fullest. The voyage on the *Lusitania* had been their honeymoon.

Days had passed in which she had anxiously tried to persuade herself that she might still get a cable announcing their rescue. After all, many survivors had been seriously hurt, and, she imagined, might be lying unconscious in an Irish hospital. Finally, she had no option but to face her loss – both Nettie and Thomas had been officially counted amongst the dead.

It was only then that she allowed herself to confront the facts. It seemed the passengers had been at luncheon; some had already finished. The *Lusitania* was within ninety miles of the Irish coastline and because submarines had been sighted here and there, there had been a strict look-out, although the general consensus had been that there was nothing to fear, the *Lusitania* was one of the fastest vessels built, she could outrun any submarine... As the final finding put it, three torpedoes had been fired in quick succession. There was a lot of confusion as to which side of the liner was hit first; in any case, one of the torpedoes caused a horrifying explosion, portions of the splintered hull were thrown clear into the air, and the vessel listed dangerously after pitching forward, shearing the davits of the lifeboats which made the lifeboats useless on that side. No warning had been given and the ship had carried no arms, officials insisted.

It was a sad fact that very few first class passengers had been saved. They had been too convinced of their invulnerability and had relied too much on their faith in the wonders and advances of technology. They seemed to have truly believed that technology itself would work for their side alone.

At home she found that Daniel, Daniel McCreedy, her fiancé, had written. Two letters at once, highly unusual for him. She opened them up and arranged them by date; they were written a day apart.

For the last three years she and Daniel had studied psychology at the University of Toronto. Both had been considered excellent students, mature and serious. Nobody had been surprised when their constant togetherness had evolved into courtship and, at their graduation, as if to celebrate their achievements, into an engagement. Like Caitlin's father, Daniel's father was a doctor and their paths might have crossed sooner or later anyway, given the social circles they moved in. People frequently commented on what a handsome couple they made. In fact, it would have been difficult for either of them to imagine any area of major disagreement between them that could not have been settled in a civilized way and manner.

When it came time to apply for their qualifying year, both had applied to Mercy Hospital in Boston. When Daniel was accepted, she remembered considering this part of the natural order of things. Sensibly, they had agreed to put the time apart to good use. He would try and make the necessary connections to set themselves up for a married and professional life together, while she, after having found her present position at the Toronto Hospital for the Insane, basically as a result of her father's good name and the mentorship of Dr. MacLean, would gain the necessary accreditation and experience. This was the plan.

In the meantime they wrote letters. Hers were filled with news from home, anecdotes about her work, her doubts and observations. At times they were more a journal to herself than a letter to a fiancé. His were brimming over with tasks accomplished, people met, hints of success in the making. He wrote very little of what she really wanted to know: what he observed, felt, lacked or ached for. She tried to tell herself that even in person, reading Daniel's feelings was more a matter of perspicacity on her part, than any expression of feelings on his side. She had teased him about that often enough, but their letter-writing had brought the problem into sharper focus.

Today's letter, the first one, touched on their relationship fleetingly in its salutation "My dear Caitlin" and just as fleetingly in its closing "Your loving Daniel;" in between he gave a recital of social events, important connections having been made, departmental politics having been decoded and mastered...four densely written pages of it. The second letter was mercifully short and contrite, expressing remorse at his "useless and unfeeling" letter of the day before. "Please ignore it," Daniel pleaded, and "I'll make it up to you when I finally see you again..."

Caitlin sipped her tea, folded both letters into one envelope and thought – which one is real? Which part of me, which image of me is he engaged to and what have I committed myself to? Wearily she decided to shelve the answers for a while. Instead, she let herself a bath, her own hydrotherapy. No wonder that being immersed in the sensuous, enveloping warmth of water could quiet down even the insane, for a while.

When she woke up the next morning and opened the curtains, the garden had been transformed. Seemingly overnight the apple tree at the back of the garden had blossomed, drawing the eye to the pale-pink clusters that garlanded each branch. Every year she was struck again by the fragility of those blossoms that were subject to the vagaries of the weather; too much heat, too much wind, or a rain storm could put an end to it all. This first blossoming always triggered memories of her mother. No wonder she shied away from the garden, preferring to enjoy it from a distance. Mrs. Harris was used to it by now. She seemed to sense that Caitlin could only take the garden when physically removed from its fragrances, its tactile beauty, its continuous evocation of the past.

¤

Caitlin was glad that she had made plans for the whole weekend. Matthew, her cousin Sybil's husband, would be sending the car to pick her up. Syb had complained humorously that they had not seen her all winter and that she had to rely on meeting her at parties or concerts. And in fact, the last time they had met, Syb had still been pregnant with the new baby. Caitlin definitely had to visit, see them, see the children, let them spoil her with their domesticity. She could almost hear the old undercurrent of "poor Caitlin, all alone in that big house" that had followed her for years. Yet now she was glad she had accepted their invitation. They lived west of the city, at the Humber. It would be a country excursion. It would be a way of fighting the past with the present.

The Humber Valley still looked the way the Don Valley must have looked a little while ago. The river had a meandering, artless quality; one could follow its course on narrow footpaths. Clusters of willows, catkins and poplars grew along its borders, wildflowers along the banks; walking there soothed her spirit.

Matthew and Syb had settled into a charming house with the air of a cottage and the amenities of the city. Syb, as energetic as ever, slim again and healthy-looking, drew her into the garden where they had set up a luncheon table in a copse of trees. She told Caitlin that since it was a country garden they had decided to let nature dictate its shape, form and purpose. No English lawns for them, no formal flowerbeds, they just wanted a refuge.

It felt good being with them and soaking up their contented domesticity. The intermittent sounds of adult laughter, a child's voice, a baby's small animal noises, everything seemed in gentle harmony with this pastoral setting. How easy it was to lose track of the fact that this is what life ought to be: find someone to love, have children, become a family, nurture another generation, pass something on of who you are. Yet in a way, it was the simplest and most challenging task of all.

To her surprise she found herself returning to this visit with Syb's family several times over the next few days. She wondered whether it was her work that accounted for this pull of the past, or was it because she had on the whole successfully avoided remembering? In any case, quiet moments tended to snag her and return her to the most painful memory of her childhood.

Caitlin was eight years old – in a few weeks it would be Christmas. Her father had been to a medical conference in Montreal and had persuaded her mother to come along to see old friends and tour the city. They were going to come home that evening. Her mother had promised her that she could help in getting the house ready for the holidays after her return. She had missed her mother's carefree laughter and her father's reassuring voice, just as she had missed the ebb and flow of their presence in the house.

Mrs. Harris had bustled about more than usual, arranging and rearranging things. Finally, Mr. Harris, coachman, gardener, general factotum, had left to pick up her parents at

Union Station. Outside, dusk was settling in. The neighbours' lights glowed here and there, easily seen now that the trees were bare; and big, soft snowflakes, the first snowfall of the season, were beginning to cover up the walkway. Mrs. Harris knew enough about children, and Caitlin in particular, that putting Caitlin to bed now was impossible and unthinkable.

Caitlin had busied herself as much as possible given her anticipation. She had drawn pictures, one for each parent and one for both of them. She had helped set the table and hung around the kitchen, asking more questions than she usually asked in a month. Yet time refused to move on. Each time she had wandered past the grandfather clock (whose grandfather, she often wondered...) she was startled to see that the hands of the clock had hardly moved.

Eventually she must have fallen asleep on the sofa. When she woke up, she felt disoriented and confused by the feel of her mother's afghan covering her and the deep dark silence in the house. Mrs. Harris appeared to put on the light in the alcove and to tell her that her parents had been delayed, and that she would take her to bed and wake her when they came home. Caitlin was too sleepy to argue and let herself be tucked in.

When she awoke it was morning. She realized Mrs. Harris had forgotten to wake her! It was a clear, bright morning with all the magic of freshly fallen snow. Excited she ran to her parents' bedroom. Their bed was untouched, the drapes drawn back, to let the sunlight flood the empty room with merciless clarity. She flew down the stairs shouting, "Where are they?"

Mrs. Harris, looking as if she had not slept at all, said "Caitlin dear, I have something to tell you," and after what seemed like an eternity-filled pause, "There's been an accident, a collision, a train wreck, people have been killed...your parents too." As she embraced Caitlin, she could smell lilac, Mrs. Harris's lilac soap, and she could feel Mrs. Harris's tears on her own cheeks, wet and foreign.

The hours and weeks after that stuck together in her mind like a glutinous mass. The house seemed dulled by silence, except for the clock's merciless accounting of the hours. Colours seemed muted, routine a sham, just another way to get through the day until sleep would release her. She insisted on eating her meals in the kitchen with the Harrises, anything, not to have to face the dining room by herself. Caitlin remembered various relatives patting her, stressing what a "brave girl" she was, "so sensible." School was what saved her, having to be there and needing to concentrate on her work and the well-loved routine of riding in the carriage to get there. She remembered the sight of the untouched snow early in the morning, the bracing air, the small clouds of breath puffing from the horse's nostrils when it greeted her each morning, and the feel of the plaid on her knees to be replaced on really cold days by the fur throw. She remembered all that, and Mr. Harris's unfailing kindness and even disposition.

Yet the year remained fractured in her memory. She could not remember Christmas for instance; she probably spent it at Syb's house. Her aunt would have invited her for the Christmas holidays. She could almost hear her reasoning: "Let her be with the children, let her play and forget..." In any case, after the holidays, Aunt Nettie moved in.

Aunt Nettie had tried hard, and so had Caitlin. Yet she always seemed aware of that small voice inside her head that whispered, "You have to be good, brave, smart and agreeable, so that your parents can be proud of you..." From today's vantage point, it looked to her as if her motto had been to live in "her parents' eye" rather than God's. She seemed to have believed deep down that their hypothetical approval of her meant that she was still in some way basking in their love.

¤

As part of her rotation Caitlin was off work for two days. She decided to take a long walk through the Rosedale Ravine to the Don flats. She and Nettie had gone there often when she was younger. A path meandered conveniently close to their house down into the valley. The day was hot and she brought her broad-brimmed straw hat to keep comfortable. The valley itself was cool and comforting, only the occasional glimpse of roof lines through the thick canopy of the trees reminded her that she was still in the city. At the end of the valley the path forked. She decided to follow the Don River south to Riverdale Park. As she turned, she was startled to see the metal grid of the Prince Edward Viaduct to her left. It was still new enough as not to be permanently engraved on her mental map. Its graduated iron curves, stone abutments and supports tied one side of the valley in a pleasing, yet implacably utilitarian way, to the other side, along Bloor Street.

The flats were just that, a broad valley running north and south to accommodate the Don River flowing placidly, accompanied by willow and scrub, until it met up with the lake a few miles further south. As she got closer to the park she could hear occasional cheers and cries coming from what seemed to be a large crowd of people. When she got closer, she found hundreds of people clustered on the hill in a state of agitation – it turned out, there was going to be a hanging that morning. After asking around, she found out that a Frank M. had killed a policeman and was about to be hanged for it. Some people claimed to have seen him at one of the windows of the jail that could be seen from the park. It was the raucous cheering and booing of the crowd that she had heard from afar. There were at least five hundred people assembled here, whole families had come, and Caitlin gathered from their fractious comments that some were there because "the bastard would finally get what he deserved," while others were there to protest the inhumanity of death by hanging, advocating instead that death by electrical current would be much more humane.

The next morning the *Globe* reported that the hanging had taken place as scheduled and that it took Frank M. fifteen minutes to die – no doubt satisfying proponents on both sides of the argument.

At the Hospital, changes were in the air. Rumour had it that Superintendent Foster was going to head the new hospital in Whitby, east of the city, right on Lake Ontario. Rumour also had it, he would take almost half their patient population with him. Perhaps, finally, some of the renovations decided upon after the big debate of 1906 whether to tear down the Hospital or renovate it, would be realized. Following logically, speculations were rife as to who would succeed him here at the Hospital and whether the staff would be reorganized as well. Clearly, there was enough fodder for several rumour mills.

When Caitlin had first come to the Hospital she thought she had been realistic about how difficult it would be for her as a professional woman to be accepted into the male world of the Hospital administration. She had hoped to make her way by force of merit, allowing for a steady but persistent climb to the point where she would eventually be given her 'due'. She knew of the fate of women in psychology: barred from research universities, women still suffered from the notion that the female brain and science did not mix, that they were essentially incompatible. As a compromise, women were shunted into a few limited research topics. A woman's experience was implicitly judged inferior to a man's, since male experience was used as the yardstick for all of human experience, the norm against which a woman's must invariably fall short. Subsequently, women had earned their doctorates in "safe" areas like perception, attention and memory, where measurement was important, as if to ensure that women's perceived lack of objectivity would not influence and distort the accumulating data in the fledgling field of psychology, which, after all, aspired to being considered one of the sciences. Caitlin, who firmly believed in the efficacy of many small steps leading to a goal and had taught herself to be patient, also realized that being young and attractive created yet another barrier, since "marriage and career" were considered to be natural opposites in male minds.

Her superiors, it seemed, were satisfied that by the very act of hiring her, they had given testimony of their openness and had paid lip service to the changing times. But Caitlin had become increasingly aware of the subtle exclusionary tactics of a closed system. The male staff, while personally courteous and invariably paternalistic, had found different ways to exclude her. All too often meetings were held without her, decisions made filtered down to her through secondary channels, accompanied by Matron's somewhat smug comment, "I thought you had been told…" While Caitlin had addressed these concerns with Dr. MacLean, still the most sympathetic and open-minded of her colleagues, she found his apologies and reassurances increasingly difficult to accept. His explanations always referred to her junior status, never to her sex, but she knew that male staff members just as junior were inducted quite painlessly, while she was left to flounder at the very edge of the system and her field.

Thankfully, she had found her involvement with the schizophrenic population at the Hospital, and her individual cases in particular, rich in material, and she knew that her detailed notes would lend themselves one day to writing up her attempts at a "talking cure." Here, Dr. MacLean encouraged her. Caitlin caught herself wondering, did he want to keep her busy? He had hinted, however, that if she wished to see her work in print, it might be wise to hide her identity behind the anonymity of initials in front of her surname.

In the meantime, she found herself using her outsider status to observe and learn. It seemed a definite advantage at times not to be a player, not to be caught up in the frenzy of internal politics; it seemed to leave her more time for the things that really interested her. Philip, for instance. Just today she had received a much delayed summary from his first hospital stay in England where Philip had been sent after his breakdown. It made painful reading. According to oral reports, he had started out well enough by documenting the orderly arrival of the troops in various small French towns, the building of pontoon bridges, cavalry deployments in villages, trenches being dug, soldiers charging, lines of enemy captives being made to carry the wounded. Shortly after that he appeared to have focused more and more on the devastated bridges, the ransacked earth, bloated horse carcasses and time after time on churches and cathedrals bombed down to their foundations... And one day, apparently out of the blue, he had refused to pick up the camera and stopped communicating.

Returning home, she felt embraced by Mrs. Harris's unflagging routine, the comforts of her well-ordered existence. Never having been confronted with the everyday choices and economies that most people had to make, she was well aware that she lived in a cocoon of privilege. How often had she observed other women lining up in front of stores, pushing prams, carrying groceries, working at menial jobs? However, her own cocoon was not only safe, providing her with the necessities of life and more, but it also kept her from being part of the ebb and flow of the vibrant stream of life that she sensed existed not far from her front door.

Folding her monogrammed linen napkin and pushing it through her monogrammed sterling silver napkin ring, she would get up to walk off this nameless dissatisfaction. At times, she found herself in front of the collection of family photographs, silver or velvet framed, that were the only remaining link to her parents. Here they were, forever young and carefree, walking across the downs in England; or by the lake with her own small, dark-eyed presence nuzzled protectively between them. There was also a studio portrait of her mother in a splendid, elegant gown, her trailing hemline arranged fold by fold for posterity as if every line mattered aesthetically. The vibrant person inside was almost negated by the jewellery, the lace, the sumptuous material and its immaculate workmanship. As her eyes roamed from one photograph to another, she noted the strangely vacant stare of the women in these daguerreotypes, their tentative smiles, their unnatural gravity, and thought that, for all her stepping out into a mainly male world, she herself would fit right in with the women in these photographs. A discomfiting thought. She decided to practice her Satie pieces instead.

¤

Today, riding along Queen Street, she found herself recalling a strange and puzzling dream she had had that morning…it had been some sort of festive occasion, a large room, perhaps their dining room. The table was set with a white tablecloth, its beautifully embroidered hem fell all the way to the ground, silver candlesticks were everywhere, an ornate centre piece decorated the table, but there was no food. Her parents were there, dressed all in black, as if in mourning. It seemed to be a special occasion and she was at the centre of it – perhaps they were about to celebrate her engagement. As she turned to Daniel to introduce him to her parents, he was not there. She started looking for him, searching one room after the other in mounting panic. Finally she headed for the front door, opened it, and faced a black, starless night.

The more she dwelled on these images, the more perturbed she felt: black and white, sorrow and joy, death and life. It seemed as if there was black mourning sadness rather than white wedding joy. Could it be that she would have preferred not to have had to introduce Daniel to her parents? Was she afraid her parents would not have approved had they known him – and worse, did she herself perhaps not approve of her choice? Was facing "nothing" better than facing "something" that was not right? Too many disturbing questions to be solved in one streetcar ride. What she needed was more control over her dream life!

Caitlin was jolted back to reality by the streetcar's shuddering halt. As happened all too often there was yet another delay; an automobile had stalled on the tracks. Before she knew it, some of the more energetic passengers had got off the streetcar to help with pushing it off the tracks on to the side of the road. Another small event that could be verified in tomorrow's newspaper, under the heading of "streetcar delays." It always puzzled her the way the papers noted the exact number of minutes a streetcar had stalled, when the event itself in all its inconsequentiality had long ago receded into the humdrum of the past. Why did it seem so important to record these small bits of mechanical breakdown in the increasingly automated flow of modern life, she wondered?

As she entered her office that morning she found a note from Dr. MacLean to see him at ten o'clock in his office. He wanted her to meet someone. "Meet Dr. Sparshott," he said when she came, "practically your predecessor, Caitlin, he is now at the new College Military Hospital, in what used to be Bishop Strachan School – that's right, you used to go there. Dr. Sparshott works with the increasing number of veterans that suffer from various shock symptoms, even though they have now returned to their, one would hope, quiet civilian lives. However, it is becoming apparent that many more young men are afflicted, and more severely, than all of us had previously thought. In fact, we find that quite a few of them cannot pursue their old vocations, or pick up their lives where they had left them four years ago." Then turning aside, he said, "Joshua, you are in a much better position to explain to Dr. Winstrum what you hope to do…" Caitlin listened attentively to Dr. Sparshott's impassioned description of their program and, in the end, agreed to come and visit the Military Hospital to see for herself.

The evening felt the way a summer evening ought to feel. She had decided to walk home by way of the Campus. Crossing the large green in front of University College and perhaps mindful of the conversation with Dr. Sparshott, she suddenly remembered the beginning of the war. She recalled in particular the morning when, going to classes, she had come across an unfolding sea of small circular tents on the green in front of University College. When they were all set up, their orderly arrangement and festive white had made them look from afar as if one had happened on a garden party or a summer fair. For the next few months, recruitment officers had vetted the fit and the unfit here. Later, training exercises had taken over, and somewhere along the way, the 'green' had died, so much so, that now the grounds would need a complete resodding.

In retrospect, it seemed strange how, in spite of the war, their privileged student lives had just gone on without missing a beat. They had felt themselves insulated by class and education. Of course a few students had signed up and were considered by the rest of them to be "too idealistic, too patriotic," perhaps even lacking in essential self-interest. For her, and the few other women on campus, the question naturally never had come up. She remembered the parade down University Avenue and the crowds at Union Station that waved the recruits off with muted enthusiasm (nothing like the festive air at the beginning of the Boer War). But on the whole, the war was "over there," its full impact cushioned by initial euphoria and the belief that it would be over shortly. In many ways it had seemed like just another opportunity for heroic action, another confirmation of the invincibility of the British Empire. She remembered taking it in, as if on the very periphery of her visual field.

A few young men from her own background had enlisted, like her friend Bella's fiancé, and a distant cousin of hers, but the full impact, like a delayed charge, was felt only now, after the return of the veterans. Every day, the newspaper carried stories of veterans hanging themselves in the woods, shooting themselves in rooming houses, killing their families and then themselves. And only yesterday, she overheard the nurses discussing the trial of a young woman who had apparently killed her newborn, stuffed it up the chimney in a desperate act of concealment before her husband's return from the war the following day. The nurses, young, and despite their job, easily shocked when something happened in real life, had stressed that the young mother's neighbours had alerted the police and had claimed that the father of the baby had been another soldier.

Sometimes it seemed to her as if the ground was shifting, as if the old moral values were about to become undone and only the ones willing to change would "inherit the earth." Something seemed to have cracked wide open over there in the battlefields, and they were only beginning to feel the after-shocks now.

Philip sat quietly in his seat. Only his hands ran slowly along the edge of the desk, while his eyes focused on the small bunch of wildflowers in the water glass in front of them. Caitlin had picked them impulsively on her way to work, they were nothing special: some daisies, a few heads of clover, different grasses. "Did you pick them?" "Yes." He looked at her with wonder and a brief surge of interest, then he bent over to pull out a head of clover and plucking out two or three small bracts of the clover head, he started sucking at their ends. "Did you ever do that when you were a kid?" he asked. "I don't think so," she answered, "Tell me about it…" Briefly, a door seemed to have opened on a personal reminiscence, but only briefly, and then it closed again, as if he lacked the effort to keep it open, or he realized the futility of trying to pursue it. Instead, he slid clear away from her presence back into his own reality.

At times, she experienced this abandonment of consensual reality as an almost deliberate act on his part; at others, she felt he must be as lost as he made *her* feel.

¤

Caitlin's work at the Hospital had found the comforting groove of a routine, if life in a hospital for the insane could ever be called routine. As Matron had pointed out, there were days and nights when what happened did honour to the old terms of *bedlam* and *lunatic asylum*. As proud as all of them were of not using the kind of physical restraints from of old, Matron admitted that the use of alcohol to quiet down excitable temperaments, "as warranted," was almost routine. Yet, this was a far cry from the times when the yearly bills for alcohol had exceeded those of any other medication! Now, as she knew, they tended to rely mainly on the curative effects of continuous tepid baths. Yes, Caitlin had been surprised when she first came to see patients dozing, immersed up to the neck in a bathtub. The tiled rooms had been flooded with sunlight; no doubt the windows had been wide open as well. She could still see the blinding white sheets draped over the white bathtubs, the nurses all dressed in white as well, the gleaming tiles on the walls and the black and white checkerboard of the tiled floor. In that light everything had a hyper, almost unreal sheen. Only the gentle murmur of water flowing through the hoses broke the silence.

Some time ago, during a brief lull in their day, Matron had talked to her of earlier, more brutal methods and had taken her on a quick tour and demonstration. Shuddering, Caitlin recalled small trunk-like cages made out of wood, called "cribs," and upright wooden stalls, just tall enough for a man or a woman to stand in. What struck her as most medieval of all were the clumsy-looking wooden chairs with a leather strap across the chest to keep the person upright, and a wooden board across the lap to hold manacled wrists in place while leather cuffs encased the arms almost to the elbow to prevent self-mutilation. These "engines of restraint," as they were called, seemed to her to come straight from a torturer's imagination, yet here they were, their wood worn smooth, scratched and abraded below the stain, scarred by use.

These days, if neither alcohol nor hydrotherapy worked, there were always camisole restraints, or if need be, full body restraints, that wrapped the whole body in canvas, like a shroud, and laced up the centre of the body so that only the head was left free. When Caitlin had commented on beds that had a full-length metal cage attached over top, their ribs just wide enough apart to feed someone, Matron had nodded, "Yes, of course, as warranted."

On the whole, and especially depending on which ward you were on, you could forget at times where you were. The builders had strongly believed in letting light enter the dark ages of the treatment of the insane. Large multi-paned windows, shuttered on the inside to filter the light as needed, were everywhere. The long and exceptionally wide corridors ended here and there in screened, curved verandahs where patients could sit and take in the fresh air, because air, aside from proper lighting, was considered to be curative by itself. These long hallways with their ceiling fans, potted plants, assortment of cushioned, comfortable wicker and rocking chairs, their oil paintings on the walls and small tables scattered about, could make you think on a good day that you were walking the halls of one of the great ocean liners, except that, as a rule, this particular voyage could take years and take you right up to your death.

Making her rounds today, she passed the young woman who spent her days sitting on the floor, her skirts swept over her head, hiding most of her body. Caitlin could never remember her face, since it would only appear briefly with a dazed look when someone insisted she sit "properly," only to disappear again seconds later as they turned their attention elsewhere. Sitting like that seemed self-protective and self-accusatory at the same time. While some patients sat chronically apathetic, others were lively, wound-up, and full of incomprehensible mirth, while others yet were known to call out to you the latest revelation from another world. The sheer number of patients in the wards and their emotional inaccessibility had overwhelmed her at first. She told herself she needed to become realistic about what she could accomplish, what her job demanded and what its limits were. Yet it was a daily struggle, one in which Dr. MacLean's Friday morning observations had been extremely helpful. His unwavering, stoic, even cheerful, acceptance of the variety of human misery had so far not sapped his energies, or his will to be useful.

Seeing her individual cases had been helpful. They anchored her, allowed her to focus and to learn. Take Philip, for instance. He seemed to make some progress, had days when she could engage him for a time, until he slipped away from her in a few well-practiced moves. The nurses had told her that he seemed to be more aware of the days when the two of them would meet and that he even appeared to check the time to remind them of where he had to be. On his good days, she felt they were accumulating a backlog of trust, and she was pleased to see his flickering interest, and the occasional glimmer of insight. On such days, she knew that she was reaping the reward for waiting in silence and being sensitive in her timing. It seemed as if a series of steps were being choreographed in the space between them until they became second nature, felt comfortable and could be built on. The very regularity of their sessions produced a sense of time's passing. A sense of a definable past and palpable present characterized their meetings and allowed, by implication, for a sense of the future to unfold.

Throughout the summer, her morning reading of the *Globe* had been about the '*Huns*'. The Versailles Peace Treaty terms were being hammered out, yet the shrill propaganda of war continued seemingly unbroken. She realized of course that an enemy that had been cultivated for some years could not so easily be given a human face after the hostilities on the battlefield had ceased, but she felt increasingly uneasy about the simplistic differentiation into black and white, good and evil. After all, had they not also read about the spontaneous ceasefire on Christmas Day 1914, when both sides had laid down their arms, embraced and even exchanged gifts person to person? She knew such thoughts were best kept to oneself in the light of what came later, but a deep distrust of oversimplification made her fold up the paper.

One day, recently, she had received a long, chatty letter from Bella, Crystabel Howard, their long-time neighbour at her parents' cottage in Muskoka. Bella chided her for never being seen in the "right places," so that she had no option but to write her. She went on for several pages in her humorous, slightly whimsical style. Nothing, as far as Caitlin had been able to discover, was ever serious for Bella, or held her attention for too long. It seemed the summer at the Howards' was going to be another busy one. Their various guest cottages and their own house of course, were already overflowing with the "most amusing" summer guests, who from Caitlin's perspective shifted like sand dunes but provided endless grist for Bella's satirical tongue. "Try and come at least once before the end of the summer, we need another pretty young woman here to keep all the idle young men interested," she had written. "In any case, you *have* to be there for our Summer's End Party!"

Caitlin had planned on going to the cottage for some time, and Bella was right, she had not made room for much else in her life except work. Her personal life had seemed on hold.

¤

It was a beautiful fall day when Caitlin finally made her way towards the Howards' cottage. Her usual reluctance to socialize had her wondering why she bothered with all these people she hardly knew, but perhaps that wasn't quite truthful; she did know them, from past summers and too many similar occasions. She hoped that one or two kindred spirits would make it all worthwhile.

It was already getting dark. She smiled to herself; how typical for her this late entrance, as if she was hoping the party had wound down by the time she arrived. Through the trees she could see the main house perched up on the cliff, every room lit up, blazing like an ocean liner ready to be launched. She could almost hear Mrs. Howard's voice turning away the inevitable compliments on the majestic view, with her dry, "You know my husband. He'll do anything for a fine view..." Caitlin was always surprised by the level of suggestiveness in Mrs. Howard's voice. Come to think of it, Mrs. Howard must have been a young Bella once.

Inside, the party was in full swing. Every room seemed to vibrate with music, voices, and laughter. After having greeted her hosts, she found Bella by making straight for the most animated group. She decided it was probably good for her to creep out of her hermit's shell at least once in a while.

Bella gushed and embraced her while looking around for her fiancé. "You were at our engagement party, you have met Martin, haven't you?" In fact, she had not been at her engagement party but had met Martin, once, briefly, as part of Bella's usual coterie on the dock. She vaguely remembered an upcoming young lawyer, articulate and energetic. In any case, Martin was nowhere to be seen; he seemed to have been swallowed up by the ebb and flow of this hectic tide of humanity bent on enjoying itself.

Much later she decided to step outside on the porch to catch a breath of fresh air and soak up the star-filled dark. It seemed others had had the same idea. There was a small group sitting in the deep wicker chairs, a few people were sprawling on the stairs leading to the garden, and others sat on the broad balustrade. Her first impulse was to step back, but it was too late; one of them got up without a word and offered her his chair. She felt it would have been rude to decline. When she settled down, she realized that they had been quiet because someone was telling a story, a personal story, to judge by the small catch in his throat. For some reason the young man's story had stopped the usual high-spirited banter; his voice was low, insistent and, she realized, full of pain.

Caitlin needed a few minutes to find her bearings, having missed the beginning. Apparently he had recently returned from the war, had been discharged in July and after a few days in Toronto, had gone home to the east coast. Having missed almost four years of his life, he was eager to see his family, in particular his two younger sisters who had been just kids when he left and now one of them was married already.

The unknown narrator mused how at first everything had seemed the same, as if time had stood still in the intervening four years; and yet, in other ways, nothing seemed quite the same to him. After his experiences in France and Belgium, the most ordinary things took on an unlikely air. His sisters, for example, suddenly looked and acted very much like young ladies; the older, Eloise, was to all appearances completely absorbed in her newly married state. He had decided to stay at the house for awhile; it would buy him time to think about his future and help him map out a plan for himself. While in the trenches, and later at the hospital, he had never once allowed his thoughts to stray into a definable future. All that had mattered then was to survive.

Back home, feeling himself loved and appreciated and with a timeless stretch of hours and days in which to enjoy just being back, he had fallen into a pleasant routine, almost a return to childhood with no responsibilities. Now that he knew some people in Toronto and had been abroad, he felt he could allow himself to explore a future that had a wider horizon than their small community would have allowed.

Yet, one morning – during his third week home – he was awakened by loud voices downstairs; next he heard his mother's running footsteps on the staircase and an urgency in her voice that made him jump. She entered his room utterly distraught. Groping for words she just pulled him with her towards the other part of the house where his sister and her husband were living until they could find a place of their own. By now his mother was sobbing. He could make out Eloise's name and knew that something terrible must have happened.

When he tried to recollect afterwards what had taken place, when he tried to put the pieces into some sort of causal sequence, he would remember the feel of the china door knob, cool and impersonal in his hand before he opened the door. He could see himself standing in the door frame, and after his eyes had adjusted to the early morning half light, he made out his sister's figure on the bed. She was wearing a long night gown, white cotton with something frilly at her wrists; her hands lay primly by her sides, her feet were half covered by a blanket as if to keep them warm, and her hair, her beautiful, reddish-brown, wavy hair, was spread all over the pillow and over her shoulders. What he struggled with was the part that defied description; her face was covered by the blind stare of a gas mask, his own gas mask most likely. His sister had pulled that awful, inhuman, face of war over her own face, blotting out her quizzical blue-green eyes, the freckles that speckled her nose, her still round cheeks and her habitual shy smile.

He could not touch that rubber mask and had to turn away when someone else, apparently the doctor who had finally arrived, removed it. He had no awareness as to how long he had sat there, one of his hands resting lightly on hers, minutes, hours, filled with an eternity of feelings. A day later, the newspapers had summed it up saying: "...used her brother's gas mask to commit suicide...had spread handkerchiefs soaked in chloroform over her face, put on the mask...was found cold in death the next morning." This was followed by speculations about a nervous breakdown, or temporary insanity. "Temporary insanity," he heard himself say bitterly. In any case, that was why he was back here. His sister's death had made the decision for him. He needed to go far away from anyone he loved after having brought death into the house and spreading it like an infectious disease.

A group of people inside the house must have shifted. Their moving bodies on the other side of the windowpane suddenly unblocked a source of light and flooded the porch. Like a searchlight it tracked across their group, trapping their stunned faces. Briefly, it caught a young man's hand – Bella's fiancé's? – on the narrator's sleeve, and just as briefly his eyes held her own, then the dark returned and each was left alone with the story.

¤

Martin woke up stifling a scream. He felt as if he was crawling back up to the surface of reality as if out of a deep crater. He felt sluggish and panic-stricken at the same time. Again he had dreamt that his lower legs were encased in mud as if in cement, he was drenched in sweat, his heart pounded, he knew that a return to sleep would be impossible. He fumbled for the light switch, to be saved once again by the sanity of light. Struggling to his feet, he needed the solid confirmation of the wooden floor under his feet and to see the familiar arrangement of the furniture. Cool nighttime air hit his face as he found and opened the door to the porch.

Would the war never end? The moment he closed his eyes, seeking oblivion, disturbing images returned and wrought havoc. Surely he deserved a good night's rest as much as anyone. As his fears cooled off in the night air, he realized that the stimulation of the party – too many people, too much drinking, too much of everything – had stressed his system rather than relaxed it. And then that story. That nightmare vision of the young woman choosing to die wearing her brother's gas mask, that story had not helped. Briefly the last scene presented itself to him once more: the painful silence after his friend Jake's voice had trailed off, the sudden beam of light on their faces, their emotions caught unawares when they were at their most vulnerable – and then the face of Caitlin Winstrum. There had been so much feeling, such rich emotion in her eyes, sadness, horror and compassion, all in one. He searched for his cigarettes, anything to calm this edginess, soothe his strained nervous system. Sitting on the steps, he made himself listen to the sounds of the night and concentrate on the rhythmic slapping of the water against the dock. He needed to anchor himself somewhere, here, in the north, here in Canada, almost a year after the war had finally been declared as won.

The worst of it was that his thinking had taken on a terrible circularity when he allowed his thoughts full rein. No matter where he started, he invariably ended up in the horror-stricken terror of the war. Scanning the darkness around him, his eyes were drawn to a flickering light in the trees; someone else was awake, in the Winstrum's cottage on the far hillside.

Caitlin had been roaming the length and width of the cottage, wandering about with a somnambulist's certainty. With only the weak light from the open bedroom door, she decided to light the oil lamp on the verandah as well. No use fighting it, sometimes it seemed easier to give in to sleeplessness. She was used to turning on the light in order to banish the dark pull of dreams, or, equally disturbing, that leaden feeling of something waiting to be acknowledged, wanting to be named. During the day this was one of her favourite places. The verandah ran along the full length of the cottage, mosquito screens kept it comfortable, a motley collection of garden chairs and small tables allowed for many different activities. She liked the feel of the grass matting under her feet, the faded chintz cushions, each one like one of the soft sepia daguerreotypes of her childhood. She carefully wrapped her morning coat around her legs, tucked one foot under and used the other to rock gently and absentmindedly in one of the old wicker chairs.

The party's heightened spirits had yet to subside in her. Perhaps it was not so much the general party atmosphere, as the time spent listening to that tragic story, actually more like a confession, that had taken the form of a tale that needed to be told again and again, as if to make it finally real and comprehensible to the teller. She had of course observed the healing power of the much-told tale again and again in her encounters with patients. Several times she had been the recipient of the terrible need to let an event recast itself over and over until one day, subtle changes in the telling, an emphasis on certain words, a new slant, allowed for the emergence of a new meaning which could finally move pain to a place of healing. And she knew about the power of hearing oneself tell one's own story, and of the power of the listener to effect change just by being there. It seemed as if, in a series of painful forays, the meaning of a life was being moved forward in time and away from the hold of the past.

Having reached this point, she realized that in some way this also applied to herself. Against the backdrop of the rhythmic creaking of the rocking chair, against the dark wash of the night, she felt a compelling comparison rise in her which allowed her to admit, for the first time, that she too had a tale that needed telling and that she needed to find words with which to confront her past. The image of the young woman's mysterious suicide would not let her go; after the shock of the 'how,' one was left with the unanswered 'why'. Is this what happened when one lost touch with one's own inner reality?

She was torn out of her thoughts by someone calling softly, "Miss Winstrum? It's Martin Rhys. I saw your light. Can I come in? Can I speak to you?"

He looked as if he had put on the first thing at hand, his black dress pants, the shirt open at the neck, the sleeves carelessly rolled back and his bare feet incongruously in his Oxfords. "I am sorry, I couldn't sleep and when I saw your light through the trees I thought 'a fellow-sufferer.' Perhaps we can talk a bit, perhaps I can talk..." With that his voice trailed off.

He sat down opposite her. The light emphasized the dark shadows under his eyes, their desperate blackness. This was not just a social call at the wrong time of the day. Before she knew it, she was saying, "Do you often suffer from sleeplessness?" He nodded and then, after a pause, "Since I've come back..." Before she could say, "And when was that?" he was already saying, "In July, this July – after three years and eight months."

"Don't ask me why I went," he continued. "I can't reconstruct that – youthful idealism, a misplaced sense of adventure, discontent with becoming a lawyer and treading the well-trodden path – I don't know anymore. In any case, there I was in France, marching into war, into battle. And don't ask me why I am here today. That is the other great mystery. At one point my friends and I were heading towards the front with a mixture of excitement and a delight in comradeship mingled with a sense of invulnerable maleness...then everything changed. I don't actually have the words for what went on over there. It seemed that while my body continued to eat, shit and ache, feel wet and cold, while my lungs filled with gas and my mouth with earth, my hands and feet were on automatic and my heart just kept pounding; yet I did not truly feel anything, or think one coherent thought."

He paused, as if to underline his incomprehension, before resuming. "Nor did I let myself measure the pitiful yards of devastated ground that were gained and lost, over and over, by the end of a day, or at the end of a battle. No, feeling was not allowed to enter into it, after seven days in the front line, seven days in the support line, or the seven days in reserve that followed. Seven whole days of being billeted meant official amnesia, an immersion in the basic care-taking functions of battered and exhausted bodies." Caitlin could see how he struggled to share an experience that was basically beyond words.

"After all that, you'd think I would be happy just to be back. Yet here I am, back in my civilian life, and everything is far from normal. It turns out nothing is truly forgotten, everything clamors to be acknowledged and even though I manage to keep the lid on all this turmoil during the day, my nights are as shell-shocked as my days used to be. I wake up drenched in sweat, my hands shake as if they had been clenched around a gun for hours and the panic that fills my chest feels as real as any while I fought in the trenches."

Caitlin said very little, knowing that he needed her to listen and be there, be the other person in this small, warm circle of light. As she continued hearing him out, his intensity and pain were palpable; she had to slow down her breathing deliberately in order to reach the calm centre in herself that allowed her to take it all in.

At one point, she found herself closing her eyes to follow him better to where he had gone. Briefly she thought: this is a part of life women have no idea of, this is one area where being female is a major advantage; it automatically excluded one from taking up a gun, from finding oneself over there, from where there could be no safe return.

When she opened her eyes again, she saw his slumped figure opposite her, both defeated and desperate at the same time; and she heard him say quietly and wonderingly, more to himself than to her, "How can one go on as if nothing has happened, how can one allow oneself to forget?" Tears were running down his face. He wiped them away with an impatient gesture that made her reach out to put her hand on his arm. As she got up and embraced him, she knew she was stepping across a line, a gulf, which until then had divided two separate existences. Yet it did not seem to matter. What mattered was the reaching out.

What happened next took place as if in another reality. She bent down to kiss his hair and he lifted his head to meet her mouth. Wanting to give comfort, she had unearthed something else. Wanting to add life to the equation that threatened to reveal the utter meaninglessness of everything, she threw her whole being into the scales.

¤

When she awoke, it came as a distinct shock to see Martin lying there, sprawled over half the bed. The light coming in still had that early dawn tentativeness. She turned fully towards him and let her eyes travel across the unfamiliar shape. Moving upwards from his narrow white feet she traveled the whole length of his body, parts of which were both hidden and revealed by the disarray of the bed covers. Right in front of her, she could skip up each small vertebra on his spinal column as if on a series of stepping-stones; on either side, his back curved and hollowed like dunes. She let her eyes wander, not wanting to disturb his sleep. Just feeling the pleasure of another body, lying so artlessly and naturally beside her, was enough.

In time, small fingers of light revealed a new topography. What had appeared at first to be fine scratch marks revealed themselves as a series of small scars, shaped as if small petals had been dropped on his back from way up high. Then she realized, a lump forming in her throat, that these were the leavings of war. Gently she lowered her hand over the area, as if its warmth could melt his injuries and negate the vulnerability of the body.

She must have fallen again into that dream-filled space that often preceded her getting up. When she woke up, she realized even before she opened her eyes that next to her was a void. He had left. She walked barefoot through every room until she came upon his note on one of the tables: "Caitlin, sorry to leave like that…come by at eleven and I'll show you what I tried to describe so inadequately yesterday."

For a long self-absorbed period she had forgotten about her plans for the day, and now she had to dress quickly. On her way through the woods to the Howards' cottage she tried to work out her feelings, realizing that she needed to protect herself in front of the world. Finally, she decided to put on her professional armour should she meet Bella's parents or any houseguests that might be about.

Rather belatedly, she noticed the unusual morning calm of the porch, the general lack of voices; only the dogs seemed to follow their instincts and habits by greeting her arrival as vociferously as ever. Mr. and Mrs. Howard, finishing a late breakfast, appeared distracted, but were unfailingly polite. After all, they were just innocent messengers, unsuspecting in the way doting parents tend to be. Yes, Martin had left; he had decided at the last minute to leave with the others on the ten o'clock boat. Bella was gone too. But Martin had left a message saying he hoped Caitlin would take the time to look at his work. The door of the cabin was open and she was welcome to browse.

He had left his cabin surprisingly tidy, considering he left on the spur of the moment. There was an envelope with her name on it that she put into her pocket, unread. Three, or four, canvasses were leaning against the wall, one small one, seemingly unfinished, on a makeshift easel. His paints were meticulously lined up on the table, his brushes stood cleaned and upright in a cup. He was there, and not there.

For a moment, she hesitated. Perhaps she would not like what she would see. Martin had prepared her for something that might not be easy to digest, something that he still felt raw and protective about. She was grateful now that he did not stand next to her, looking over her shoulder, reading her face as she tried to take in what she saw.

Carefully, she lifted each canvas and leaned it against the wall. The first things she noticed were a lot of earth tones, muddy browns, clay-reds, humus-black, dreary olive green, with occasional lighter touches of taupe or grey. As her eye focused on one after the other she realized he was right, there was nothing here to please the eye or to flatter reality. What she was looking at were a series of intersecting planes, sudden breaks, disturbing black holes, torn-up fractured matter. Used to looking for identifiable objects, she found herself casting around for analogies. She thought of swamps filled with dead trees, earth slides, earthquakes, the aftermath of a forest fire, any sort of violent destruction, until it came to her in a sudden flash of insight that this was what he had tried to describe to her when he spoke of the trenches, the mud, the destruction of meaning, and finally, the loss of reality itself. He had portrayed the devastating moment when all signs of the visible world had been annihilated and blown sky high.

The more she looked, the more she feared that beyond these disturbing abstractions she was getting a glimpse of his mind, his very soul. Here were the scars of war made painfully visible, and at that moment, she was able to forgive him for having left with the others.

When she did open the letter, it read: "Caitlin, I'm not sure I can explain. It seems important to leave, to straighten myself out, and to come to grips with the fact that I *am* alive. I think I will follow your suggestion and contact Dr. Sparshott. Thank you for everything."

The terse open-endedness of his words brought home the fact that their loving each other may have been nothing but an *escapade* on his part after all. While she had lived in the immediacy of their love, there had been no doubt, no shame, no guilt, but now all these feelings overwhelmed her and she saw clearly that they had both betrayed someone close to them. It came as a shock, how easily and naturally it could be done.

Caitlin decided to stay a few more days. It seemed important not to run. It seemed fitting to just sit on the porch. She needed this quiet time to reorganize her inner life before getting back to the world, as if she was still who she had been when she came.

On the day of her departure it had rained all night. She decided to go for a last walk in the woods nevertheless. The air smelled damp, laced with the subtle scent of decay that usually indicated the presence of mushrooms. They had sprouted seemingly overnight on the ribs of fallen logs, in groups at the bases of trees, or singly and half hidden under leaves. Rain had slicked them and they stood wet and glistening in the hush of the woods. Some leeringly suggestive, like that white, phallic-looking mushroom with its delicate fringe. The ground gave softly under her step; it had soaked up so much water that it felt like moss. Drops of water sprayed her face as they dripped off the needles and bare branches overhead. It seemed as if the birds of summer had already gone south, and all that was left was the raucous hectoring of the jays and the warning cry of an unknown bird that seemed to follow her steps by flying from tree top to tree top, as if mocking her progress.

¤

After she had come home she found a letter from Daniel waiting for her. In it he detailed the arrangements for her visit to Boston on Thanksgiving. It looked as if it would be a busy time. He wanted her to meet everyone of importance, show her Boston, and take her to the theatre, all in three days. Fortunately, it seemed there would be little time for just the two of them; for once his love of organizing would be a help rather than a hindrance. When she put the letter down she felt a gnawing sense of anger at some of the assumptions that he had made; yet on another level, she realized she had been very much a collaborator in creating these expectations. Still, it was important to go, test their relationship *in vivo* as it were, talk to a friend, resume their bond and listen to someone who had such a clear-cut sense of the future.

Back at work, she found the nursing staff huddled together. An unnatural quiet filled the hallways, as if she had walked in on the aftermath of a storm. It turned out that there had been a suicide on one of the women's wards. Betty M., a "good" patient who had had ground privileges for years, had been on her usual morning walk, which consisted mainly of circling the large flowerbed as if on a treadmill to nowhere. Or so it had always seemed to Caitlin when she observed Betty's daily rounds from her second storey vantage point. Betty was known to collect things on her walks. She picked up interesting twigs, clover leaves, small flowers, sometimes a snail, or even pieces of gravel. Today, towards the end of her walk, she had suddenly bent down and swiftly scooped up two larger stones, more rounded beach pebbles than gravel, which she proceeded to force down her throat. Apparently she had acted with such determination and speed that nobody had been able to stop her before she collapsed, letting out the most awful choking wail. No, someone else said, she had not been considered suicidal. She would not have been allowed ground privileges if she had been. Betty, it appeared, had been mending bedding in the laundry for years. She would have had plenty of opportunity to harm herself if that had been her intention. Caitlin had never seen Betty up close, but from now on she would always associate her name with the desperate woman who killed herself in such a ruthless fashion. An act that seemed less demented than sane, depending on how you looked at it.

Philip, when he came in, seemed to sense something was wrong. He paced more today, standing for a long time at the window before saying out of the blue, "Do you believe in God?" Without waiting for an answer (thank God for that!) he went on about the minister's obsession with "living in God's eye."

According to him, each Sunday's sermon over the last few weeks had been a version of the injunction to live in such a way as to be worthy of God's constant and unfailing scrutiny of each of one's actions, thoughts or desires. He returned to his seat and took up the study of his hands, turning them palm up, palm down, as if marveling at their complexity. He summed up his thoughts by saying, "Living in God's eye I can take; living in the mind's eye is what terrifies me." It seemed to Caitlin a fitting epitaph to the day.

Her Boston Thanksgiving was upon her before she knew it. On the train she felt herself rocked to sleep by the metallic, rhythmic sound of the wheels. An uneasy, fitful sleep overtook her, where the mind would not allow the body to drop deep enough to really experience forgetfulness. On waking she faced a dull November day. The dun-coloured fields outside the window were all texture, closely cropped and ragged looking. Caitlin marveled at the changes that had taken place in a few short months: how quickly the seasons had moved from the sensuous ripple of wheat, the glossy and tasselled corn rows, the cheerfulness of a pumpkin field, to this dreary scenery. Today there was so much damp November in the sky that the sun, diffused and muted, appeared to struggle to be seen.

Occasionally, drifts of Canada Geese scattered across the fields, their fawn breasts barely distinguishable amidst the stubble. At other times, the freshly turned earth attracted hundreds of seagulls, which glowed in chalk-white and dove-grey smudges against the moist brown soil. A cat-tailed marsh, a driftwood-strewn pebble beach, and, for a long time, the vistaless, leaden pewter of the lake accompanied her. Here and there small flotillas of waterfowl bobbed up and down, barely visible to the naked eye. Everything seemed shrouded in mist and uncertainty.

The first class compartment of the train was nearly empty, and was likely to stay so. She thought how easily money could secure privacy and how much she took that for granted.

The real struggle for existence took place elsewhere. Her own struggles all seemed to be internal ones. Pushed back from conscious exploration, they clamored for attention at times of quiet, or during a lull in her daily routine. Train journeys, in particular, seemed predestined to evoke the past, to turn her thoughts towards that great watershed in her childhood – her parents' death.

¤

Boston. Civilized and beautiful as far as she could make out. Three intense days of seeing and being seen. Daniel had planned it all out and Daniel's plans had a way of materializing.

Thanksgiving itself had been spent with Dr. Walmsley's family and with the other doctors from the hospital. Everyone had been welcoming and interested in her, if mainly as Daniel's fiancée. Young, pretty, well brought up, smart of course and somewhat reserved; "very Canadian" she could feel them thinking. They showed little interest in her work, offered no more than a passing acknowledgement, before they returned to their own preoccupations of hospital politics. Daniel, forever astute, already seemed to be very much an insider.

It had felt good to spend some time on herself, making herself beautiful for someone. She realized with a start that since working at the hospital her sensible outfits, mainly in shades of grey, subdued blue and occasional black, enlivened by her favourite, white, had become a professional armour of sorts. They took the focus off the comely young woman underneath. Here, for three whole days, she had slipped out of that pupa and brought only one sensible tweed outfit for traveling in; aside from that, she had blossomed into the pleasure of colour and sensuous fabrics. Dresses, shawls, matching shoes, and fancy hosiery, not just for Daniel, but also as a treat for herself.

Even her mother's jewelry had seen the light of day again. "You look resplendent," Daniel had said approvingly, putting his arm around her shoulder, as if to claim all of her. No wonder everyone just responded to the elegant young woman in her. Putting away her finery at night, she had briefly felt like Cinderella, home from the ball, the prince out of reach and both glass slippers still firmly in her possession.

Outside the train window the landscape unrolled like a carpet. Her eyes strayed along the horizon, scanning the sky in rhythm with the wheels. She was homeward bound. Her eyes were drawn to the random notation of a phalanx of Canada Geese in flight, their bodies slowly forming their signature "V" as if obeying an unseen choreographer's command. Her mind, unbidden, provided their familiar honking. Hours of unscripted time lay ahead of her, time to assess the emotional rewards of her journey. Yes, Daniel had greeted her with evident pleasure and chaperoned her from event to event with possessive fondness. He looked wonderful. She had felt a surge of love and affection as she listened to him. It was not so much what he said, but the pleasure she felt in watching him: his blue-grey eyes, intelligent and alive to the world, the decisive cut of his jaw and his quick-to-judge mouth. And she liked the way his capable hands handled things, efficient and sure of themselves, not likely to break anything. His hands tended to be quieter than the rest of him and thus spoke more of him.

At times, listening to him, she wanted to reach out and gently put her hand over his mouth to still the flow of words, the torrent of reason that seemed to come between them. But then she found herself laughing again at his ironic and apt descriptions of the world as a "work in progress." There had been too little time for just the two of them, almost as if they had conspired to have it that way. While she could read her own heart for a possible motivation, his heart was the greater mystery.

The journey through the darkening countryside had a hypnotic quality that affected her body. She was only now beginning to realize that seeing Daniel had cost her a lot of emotional and mental energy, especially the energy of concealment that accrues around any kind of betrayal. She had come to see him without any preconceived notion as to what she would share with him, as if she had hoped that his attitude might tell her how much he wanted to hear.

In the end that had amounted to nothing.

And then there was Martin. Why had she responded to him so instinctively? It was not just his vulnerability; she was exposed to that every day at work. It was more his anguish, his search, his sense that the world, cracked as it was showing itself to be, needed a totally new response. A response which he and most of his generation had not been trained for and could never have anticipated, and which they now needed to extemporize through their choices.

It was the part of him that was *seeking*, the part that questioned and the part that was willing to put himself on the line that had attracted her. A disquieting thought stirred deep inside her. She seemed to be formulating not only what had attracted her, but also what *she* wanted to become, wanted out of life, even if she never saw Martin again. A door had opened, she had stepped through it somewhat heedlessly and now there was no turning back. A thought moved deep and dark like a shadow within her. She was beginning to feel drowsy and allowed these half-formed intentions, heavy and troubling as they were, to drift back to the bottom of her consciousness.

When she had said to Dr. Sparshott that she would visit him at the Military Hospital and find out more about his project, she had followed an impulse. Now walking along College Street, entering the familiar old school building, she felt briefly disoriented. How often had she climbed this staircase in the past and felt the wooden banister worn smooth by generations of other young women? Bishop Strachan had been in many ways a life apart. How strange, that what had seemed so much a female world then, was so much a male's now. The cruel necessity of war's aftermath, the ongoing stream of returning veterans, had called for this transformation from a young woman's college to a military hospital.

As Joshua Sparshott reminded her a few minutes later: 70,000 young Torontonians went to war, and of the ones lucky enough to return (one in seven had been killed), a distressingly large number needed follow-up psychological care. He described to her his particular interest in "shell shock," or what used to be called more poetically "soldier's heart" during the Civil War.

"Here's what we know," he had recapitulated. "A whole host of symptoms, from a pronounced startle response to tremors, aches and pains, headaches, exhaustion, nightmares, generally disrupted sleep patterns, to a loss of libido and numbed emotions, are typical for exposure to trauma. Even hysterical paralysis, overwhelming anxiety and dissociation have been noted. What most of the veterans we have seen have in common is that they cannot function well in their day-to-day lives, cannot follow, or do not want to follow, their chosen occupations anymore. Interestingly enough," he had added, "it has been found that many of these symptoms tend to show up most often when the soldiers are transferred to a hospital close to home. Obviously initially, the symptoms' main function was to get them away from combat, but once that was achieved, the patterns seemed to become more fixed."

"I think we are dealing with a serious, chronic and potentially disabling condition," he continued, "and in spite of newspaper advertisements suggesting miracle cures with the help of the 'Branston generator' for example – have you read about that ingenious device?" he smiled at her, "we obviously haven't found the right treatment yet. Where art can't succeed,

I have always believed, we are all too ready to apply techniques. And then of course, there are some physicians who insist that all these symptoms are the result of organic lesions sustained in battle, whereas I believe more and more that we are, for the most part, looking at the results of what happens when the whole system, mind and body, undergoes unbearable stress."

Listening to his passionate commitment to what he saw as both an urgent social need and a scientific opportunity, she thought involuntarily of Martin Rhys and the distraught state in which she had first come to know him. Before she knew it, she had asked Dr. Sparshott to tell her more about his treatment, his ideas and the way these interacted with his research.

When Caitlin left, she had promised him one evening per week of her time to help with the preliminary interviews, the time-consuming task of history-taking. While she surprised herself with this offer, she also thought fleetingly that she might have something to contribute, perhaps the capacity to listen or her sense of having survived losses of her own. She was not sure, perhaps there was no comparison between her own experiences and the survival of the trauma of war, but something had intervened, as if from a place of deeper wisdom, and made her volunteer.

¤

This time of the year had always been difficult for her. The pre-Christmas bustle could not be ignored; it would not let her memories hibernate, as she wished they would. Instead of enjoying her evenings in the half-dark of the sitting room, she felt very vulnerable. Mrs. Harris customarily withdrew after dinner, and the house, as much as she was usually comforted by it, increasingly exuded a strained silence, which she would break at times by playing the piano or listening to the gramophone. However, this evening she found herself closing her eyes, and the memories trickled in as if to keep her company.

It had been another dark December day like today, and although she hadn't had her dinner, someone had bundled her up in several travel rugs. She was hanging on to her beloved stuffed camel, the one Papa had brought home from one of his trips. They had told her she was going to see her cousin Syb and stay with her family for a while and wouldn't that be fun? At the curve of the road she had not been able to resist turning back for a last look at the house. It had looked like a big abandoned ark, like the one in the Bible, Noah's ark.

Syb's mother, Aunt Venetia, had been nice; she had not made her eat all her food, she had just quietly taken her plate away. Her cousins had been very noisy. They didn't know about things. At night, when she woke up in a strange bed, she could hear Syb's regular breathing in the other one. Lying there, she often found herself staring down the dark until she could not stand it anymore and hid under her blanket and cried muffled, despairing sobs into the camel's neck.

When she had finally begun to feel part of Aunt Venetia's raucous, careless brood, Nettie came to pick her up. She explained to Caitlin that, when she returned to her own house, Mr. and Mrs. Harris would still be there, and she, Nettie, would stay with her.

Things were different with Nettie around. She did not seem to know about the "rules," and did not seem to be sure what Caitlin should be allowed to do. She kept saying, "We will work it out Caitlin, we will work it out our own way." It was Mrs. Harris who knew about the rules and just kept everything the way Mama used to like it.

For a long time Caitlin had left her parents' room the way it had always been. For years. It became her refuge. Until the day when Nettie suggested that now that she was older, she might want to move in herself. And she did need more space, for her books, her homework, her friends visiting. Although she changed very little, the room became over time more hers than her parents'. She filled it with voices and music as if to drown out her parents' fading presences.

When she had left Daniel waving good-bye at the railroad station in Boston, they had both agreed that their next meeting would be at his parents' Christmas dinner, in a few short weeks. He had been right; the weeks were being lapped up by the shortened days. December, with its hectic pre-holiday atmosphere, had thrown her right back into the busy social life of earlier times.

More and more often she found herself dressing for going out. Much like her mother, she stood in front of the open wardrobe, fingering silk, crêpe de Chine, georgette, delicate voile, trying to choose the most appropriate outfit, the right accessories. Mrs. Harris enjoyed these moments. Seeing Caitlin like that seemed to make her more hopeful that she might yet pick up the social mantle of the Winstrum's, as was her due. Caitlin had ordered a few new outfits for the season, more as a declaration of intent, than out of a great need, or desire. Doing things properly was a deeply rooted social reflex and she knew Daniel would appreciate it.

The McCreedys had a spacious house on Avenue Road. It was situated in a beautiful garden, filled with an exquisite assortment of rare and mature trees. In summer, the whole purpose of their immense and immaculate lawn seemed to be to show off their ancestors' perspicacious eye for landscaping. Her favourite was a majestic beech, whose even shape, low branches and blood-red leaves arrested the eye and could be seen to particular advantage through the French doors of the dining room.

Today, the house was filled with the woodsy smell of the fireplaces, the fragrance of fresh pine and cedar and the subtle undertones of beeswax candles. The beech stood in lonely splendour on the immense white lawn and on the table she noticed the most wonderful centrepiece of fruit: exotic pineapple, sensuous dark figs, translucent clusters of green grapes and matte, deep-blue ones that trailed from the comport, set off by what looked like hand-painted pears of the softest yellow. Seventeenth-century Dutch still-life paintings came to mind. Ivy trailed on the tablecloth and small sprigs of holly suggested the season.

The McCreedys had greeted her both fondly and formally, acknowledging her special relationship to their son, and the public occasion at the same time. They appeared to genuinely like her and seemed to believe that her orphaned status would make the transition from Winstrum to McCreedy an easy one. Daniel, contrary to his initial plan, had arrived only the day before. He joked that Boston set a different pace than Toronto and managed to imply a subtle, qualitative difference, a sort of superiority. It was understood that in this comparison home could only lose. He had affectionately appropriated her from the moment he had come to pick her up, overwhelming her with news of the latest Boston gossip, so much easier now that Caitlin knew the key players. She, in turn, found herself slipping easily into the role of the adoring fiancée, playing second fiddle to his easy assumption of being the first violin. As usual, this had the effect of turning her even more into herself.

Falling back on observation, the way she imagined a field anthropologist might watch a native ritual, seemed the only possible response. Stepping outside the action allowed for a small measure of freedom and quiet reflection. Occasionally, when moving amongst the guests, she could feel Daniel's eye on her. He would briefly scan her face as if to confirm that all was proceeding as it should. What he saw must have reassured him, as she could see by the faintest trace of a satisfied smile that played around the corners of his mouth.

As the various sizes of Minton plates changed in front of her and the array of glasses filled ritualistically, Mrs.

McCreedy's well-chosen and perfectly executed menu unrolled without a hitch, at least to Caitlin's eyes. She noticed that the buzz around the table had become an impenetrable welter of sound. Her neighbours on each side had been successfully engaged; conversation with those on the opposite side of the table had been given up under the acknowledged strain of not being able to hear one's own voice. The dessert was about to be given its due, and in the small lull between courses Caitlin thought wistfully, how useful it would be to have access to the ironic gift of an Edith Wharton; only she could have done justice to the whole range of social nuance and the lush, insinuating display of social power that unrolled here under the guise of Christmas dinner.

Having assured the McCreedys and Daniel that it had been a wonderful evening and that she did not mind being driven home by herself, she found herself rolling through the dark with a distinct feeling of relief. The fresh, bracing air outside and the moonlit glow of the snow seemed to muffle all voices of dissent in herself. What rose instead, unbidden, was the feeling of something that needed to be attended to.

Yet there was no time to attend to anything for the next two days. She and Daniel had spent time with Syb and Matthew one day and went to a dinner party on the other. The dinner had been given by old university friends of theirs; it was a lively and relaxed evening. She remembered with what fervour Daniel had championed his belief in unlimited progress and how easily he had side-stepped her concerns about the social problems all around them.

Each occasion had been successful on its own, but something would not let go of her. She tried to tell herself it had nothing to do with her meeting Martin, that that was finished, although he certainly had thrown her former expectations of herself into question. And that was the part she still needed to work out. She had become increasingly aware how she had spent much of her life as if in a dream, a dream in which she was moving, but moving to someone else's rhythm. Her own life force, she realized, had a muted quality, as if she could only perceive the pulse of the world through layers of cotton wool.

Obscurely, she sensed that she was poised to take another leap into the unknown, even if she knew nothing about what would come after.

When she did take it, she surprised herself with what deep conviction she told Daniel of her need to sever their engagement. What had seemed almost impossible to formulate before, what she had dreaded as a totally inarticulate moment on her part, found her describing her situation in a simple and straightforward language. She told him that she had done a lot of thinking over the last few months and that she had realized that she needed more time to sort out who she was and what she wanted in life. When she listened to herself describing her feelings towards him, she realized they sounded more like a sincere declaration of friendship, than a renunciation of love.

While she was talking, Daniel had looked at her less with surprise at what she said, than with surprise at the level of conviction in her voice. He had carefully set down the glass in his hand, as if stabilizing something inside himself before he spoke. He said that he felt totally unprepared for this turn of events, and yes, he felt hurt as well. Then he caught himself and said somewhat truculently, in any case, what was wrong with being friends, having specific goals, knowing what one wanted? He ended up reminding her how in the past many of these goals had seemed to be common ones.

It seemed to Caitlin that he talked on and on in order to regain composure, and she felt she owed it to him to agree when he suggested not doing anything rash, but using the next few months of their separation to reassess their relationship. Yet after he left, she felt a reckless sense of freedom devoid of the lingering sadness that usually follows the end of something.

Given what was happening in her life, she had decided to work on New Year's Eve. Having to work was going to anchor her. Not that she could not have joined in this or that festivity; Syb, for one, had warmly invited her several times. But she was still too surprised at the new turn her life had taken. She and Daniel had talked to each other once more, briefly, just before his return to Boston.

All around her, people seemed to rush about more purposefully today, as if everyone still needed to accomplish a number of things before the old year foreclosed on them. The day was cold; the sun shone almost too brightly while the snow underfoot had that slightly grating squeak that could get under your skin.

The young nurses-in-training, excited and in a holiday mood, acted much like school children before the dismissal bell rang. In their immaculate white outfits, white headdresses, they reminded her of a gaggle of geese. Anything could set them off and she felt a gulf far wider than the ten years that might have been between them. She was sure she had never been this young, this carefree, this much amused by life.

She, too, had started the day in a festive mood, a feeling that was there still, just below the surface of her professional activities. There seemed to be less to do today. Some patients had been picked up by their families; the ones that were well enough to work regularly had ground privileges, and were considered 'tractable'. Some time ago she had suggested to Matron to approach the Langleys about inviting Philip home for a weekend, or at least for New Year's Eve. Philip, everyone concurred, seemed much improved, but just now Matron had told her that his parents had sent word that Philip's mother's delicate health did not allow for the uncertainties that Philip's presence in their household might create... Caitlin worried that Philip might well interpret this as another rejection and decided to talk to him before going home, even though this was not one of their regular days.

The day had passed quickly in making her rounds and seeing her individual patients. Caitlin was surprised to see that darkness had fallen while she had been engrossed in trying to follow her patients' fantasies, musings and complaints. Yet, she still wanted to speak to Philip before leaving. He came to her office seemingly reluctantly, muttering something gruff; it sounded a lot like "… are you still here?" She tried to talk to him about his parents' message, but as much as she tried to empathize with the disappointment he must feel, she felt she sounded unconvincing, if not somewhat hypocritical.

For a few moments they looked at each other silently, as if silence was a more appropriate comment than anything else; then she heard herself say, "Philip, would you like to come to dinner and celebrate New Year's Eve together at my place?" She had barely time to work through the ramifications of what she had just said, when his slow nod and surprised "yes" locked her into her spontaneous gesture.

Matron showed only the slightest hint of surprise when Caitlin said, somewhat too breezily, "I have invited Philip Langley to my house to spend New Year's Eve with us." (us?) "I'll bring him back tomorrow when I start my shift." Then she added somewhat unnecessarily, "It seems too bad that his family does not want to give him a chance. Besides, it will give me an opportunity to form an opinion on how ready he is to leave."

In the cab, she had to fight a panicky "What am I doing?" which she tried putting to rest with a whole number of sound reasons: that Philip had never been violent, had been much improved since she first started to work with him, and that this would allow her to observe him in a more natural setting.

On arriving home she was greeted by a note from Mrs. Harris, saying that dinner was in the warming oven, she had made a special dessert to be found in the icebox, and she would return at lunchtime tomorrow. Happy New Year! Caitlin realized, with a rush, that although it was the middle of the week, it being a holiday meant that Mrs. Harris would be home with her family.

In the meantime, Philip stood quietly in the hall; he seemed to wait for directions as to what to do next. After inviting him to make himself at ease in their drawing room, she went to set another place at the table and warmed up their meal. Philip observed her coming and going in silence, seemingly taking in the details of his environment bit by bit, as if claiming the space visually. He stroked the shiny mahogany of the table top, tested two armchairs for their comfort and their view before deciding on one of them, then waited quietly and self-contained to see what would happen next.

Caitlin lit all the candles in the dining room. When Philip sat down he commented on how everything lived a "double life;" for instance, the candles which were multiplied in the windowpanes and the large mirror over the sideboard. The room looked warm and festive, the food was delicious, their wine glasses refilled themselves magically, and she found herself trying to draw Philip out. However, Philip, while more relaxed than usual, seemed to prefer to listen to her, and before she knew it, she was recounting childhood memories. They flowed easily and seemed to fill the usually silent house with the warmth of recollection.

Philip listened attentively and commented only rarely. His hands holding the glass moved about, trying to capture the flickering candlelight in the dark red wine. Occasionally he would glance up at the chandelier; his eyes appeared to be drawn to the many-faceted gleam of the crystal pendants that reflected on the ceiling, suggesting an underwater scene of magic and transformation. Caitlin followed his gaze, and feeling light-hearted and playful, rose and spontaneously unhooked one of the tear-shaped drops of crystal: "Here,

Philip, I want you to have this. Now you'll have your own prism to capture the light whenever you need it." Philip did not act at least surprised as he took the crystal from her hand with the delighted look of a child who had just been given a treasure.

Later, oblivious to the hour and not knowing whether it was still the old year or the new, she showed him to his room. He seemed dazed and pleased as she said, "We'll have breakfast whenever we find ourselves up. Good night and Happy New Year..."

As it turned out, Caitlin was up first. She dressed quickly and went downstairs to make breakfast for them. Although she had now made weekend breakfasts for a number of years, it still seemed a treat to putter about the kitchen by herself. Outside it was snowing heavily. It must have snowed all night, because the silence outside was palpable even inside the house. Nothing stirred so early on New Year's Day. There were no tracks on the roads or the sidewalks; the camperdown elm by the road, its branches heavily laden with snow, provided a beautiful and bizarre contrast to all that white.

Caitlin walked about the kitchen to heat the water for their tea. While she was rinsing the teapot, a pervasive sense of unreality took hold of her. She felt truly isolated in this house, as if surrounded and cast adrift in the all-enveloping white outside. Snowflakes fell like eiderdown and life seemed muffled and inscrutable.

She must not have heard Philip enter the kitchen because suddenly she became aware of him standing behind her. Looking up she saw his blurred outline framing hers in the windowpane. He did not reach out to touch her, but just leaned full-length against her back, quietly, mutely, the way a cat might. Caitlin was not really startled; it was more a quiet sense of shock that made her turn around slowly and, holding out the teapot, put it into his hands in one smooth and silent movement. Her "Philip, could you carry this into the drawing room?" released them both as if from a spell. When their bodies turned away from each other it seemed as if the snow outside had resumed its hypnotic fall.

Breakfast passed in small bursts of banal comments and long spells of silence. She had time to reflect briefly on her lack of good judgement in bringing him here. She could not help asking herself, "Shouldn't I have remembered that Mrs. Harris would be off?" Inwardly she was relieved that what could have been a really awkward situation had been managed, it seemed, even if only by a hair's breadth.

Luckily she remembered that Philip liked music and offered to play him a small piece by Satie. She tried to describe to him why it was so special to her, but words failed her when she tried to get across to him the depth of melancholy and yearning that this music suggested. Philip seemed pleased that she was willing to play for him and she ended up playing two of Satie's "gnossiennes," the ones she had practiced and grown to love over the summer. The strange atmosphere, the sense of things unsaid and not done, their mute relationship that seemed to exist on different levels of reality, all appeared to enrich the rendering of her favourite music. When she had finished and looked up, it did not seem surprising that Philip had tears in his eyes.

It continued to snow, gently and soundlessly, until long after their return to the Hospital. Each additional hour added to the sense of unreality. It seemed as if what was old and past needed to be covered by layer after layer of fresh virgin snow; as if, symbolically, the New Year needed to be scripted on a blank slate.

¤

The next few days Caitlin would be off work. She had accepted the invitation of a friend to join her at her parents' farm in Cedar Valley, northeast of the city. Caitlin was supposed to bring warm outdoor clothes and her skates. She remembered the frozen pond at the bottom of their property, nestled in a grove of cedars. No one would have suspected it there; it sat deep and comfortable like a glacial lake, which perhaps it was, in the hollow of the small valley, surrounded by tangled cedar brush. Her friend's parents had had the ice cleared, and lights had been strung up along the winding steps leading down to the pond. Down there, protected from the wind, and with the clear, dark, star-filled sky cupped over her, it was easy to forget her cares. She found herself gliding like a much younger, carefree self amongst the skaters.

When she returned to work, she walked into a room brimming with tension and, to make it more ominous still, the young nurses who normally gathered there seemed to scatter at her entry like a flock of birds. She tried to joke that she had not intended to break up anything, but her words fell flat as she caught their startled looks on the way out. "Has something happened?" she asked Matron, who was sitting as if deeply engrossed over her daily log. Unable to avoid answering, she replied, "Well, yes...one of our patients has died, has killed himself last night." When Caitlin looked at her questioningly, she said reluctantly, almost churlishly, "Yes, Philip Langley."

As if from far away, as if from the end of a dark tunnel, she heard herself exclaim, "No!" and then, as an afterthought, "How?" Matron seemed momentarily at a loss, then she explained, "You know the spiral staircase under the rotunda, the one that is rarely used; he must have made his way there during the night; in any case, he threw himself down the stairwell, apparently from the top floor. One of the male attendants found him there this morning. There was of course nothing more to be done. I am sorry, Dr. Winstrum, I know you really wanted to help him, but you know that for some of our patients it is just a question of *when*." A few moments later she added, "Philip left something for you; you'll find it on his bed."

For the rest of the day Caitlin had continued to go through the motions until she finally reached the safe haven of home. In the background of her awareness a dull ache had spread, as if from a wound sustained in battle, one that would only be felt much later when safety was regained. To drown out the anguished cry of "Why?" she fled into sleep as a way of buying time and oblivion.

All the next day she tortured her memory about whether she had missed any tell-tale signs of Philip's true state of mind. It was hard to escape the fact that she had last seen him after their return from the ill-advised visit to her house. Finally she decided that only one thing promised to bring her closer to an answer; she would have to make herself look at what Philip had left her. It turned out to be a package wrapped in his dark-blue muffler. Inside she found a journal, the one she had given him so many months ago, hoping that he might be inspired by its white, lined pages to bring something of his "inside" to the "outside," where he, or both of them, could unravel it further.

On top, wrapped separately, had lain her crystal, his prism.

Wanting to know and not wanting to know made her hesitate. Reading someone's journal, or diary, even with their permission, still felt like overstepping a line. Yet, she had no choice, she had to save both Philip's memory and herself.

On the frontispiece of the journal, filling the whole width of the page, was a pencil drawing of an eye. It was arrested in an unblinking stare, huge, not to be avoided. Its iris, with its myriad striations, its line-next-to-penciled-line obsessiveness, disclosed a whole world of complexity. It seemed a world in its own right. The blank pupil in its centre loomed like the black hole of existence. No light, no life ever reflected in this eye. It was truly the persecutory eye of the Last Judgement, the one that judges the Self.

The first few pages were left blank, as if he had looked at them and let silence fill line after line. Then abruptly, in the middle of one page, no month, no date, nothing to anchor oneself:

I wait and wait for the dark to lift, wait for the morning light. Wait while I eat, while I stand by the window. The light moving across the floor measures the day in eternities –

What for, I ask myself?

When you came and knocked politely and softly on the wall, I had learned to ignore such intrusions...

Today I found you out. You are waiting with me. You wait on your side of the desk, all haloed by the light, your face blanked out by my not seeing, I wait on my side of the desk, prisoner of the second hand whose soft click I feel in my body... more eternities pass... who can outwait whom?

I have more practice and nothing to lose.

I wait in the chair, trace its oak grain, feel its warmth... I want to get lost in the pattern of the carpet that fills the space between us with a labyrinth of tendrils that I cannot unravel or decipher... I listen to your voice... not the words... the voice that soothes and seems like a melody from long ago ... and I know this voice is yours; it is not my invention...

Why did you do that? Why did you set flowers between us? What did you want? What was I supposed to do with that? Clover? You ask me about clover... fields full of clover open up before me, I want to run and roll in summer before it becomes hay and fodder...

Why did you bring me flowers? Why do you pick flowers? Don't you know they die like everything else – while we sit here and wait?

*I'm **not** listening. I'm **not** coming to see you. I don't need to add your voice to the other voices. I don't need to let it tell me what to do.*

I'll curl up in my silence, stop up my ears and let my eyes stray around you and steal out the window – to the freedom outside...

Dr. W., you looked happy today, happy and young. Your voice sounded as if it skipped a beat now and then. As if something, someone, had made it happy.

It is harder to wait, when you wait alone.

I cannot move past this eye… it invades even here, it is not your *eye, not* God's, *it is the* mind's *eye – the one with the pitiless stare that extracts one's essence drop by drop. It never needs to blink, it never looks aside, it never sheds a tear in compassion, it holds you fast, rivets you to the ground of existence. An eternity is the smallest unit of time with which it measures… do I need to outwait* it?

I try not to let the world intrude. You are different, you still feel all this matters… I feel much, much older than you…

More blank pages, then…

The waiting is over, you broke the spell, pulled me into the present, the present of the senses, the clear, shiny-bright winter day, the smell and feel of cold leather, cigar smoke in the cab, the infernal noise of the combustion engine and your immediate presence.

Your house, behind the leaded glass door panels, the bevelled edges of the mirror, the etched amphora filled with etched flowers on the glass panes of the dining room door, the cold brilliance of the chandelier and the clear transparency of the wine glasses – everything so much like the house of my childhood. It, too, smelled of order and beeswax, of a silence so deep you knew the house was in mourning… I had magically, wantonly stepped back in time, as if through Alice's looking glass…

No more waiting, only the blur of the senses and warmth. The warmth of the candles, the fire, the wine, your voice and your laughter.

And the next morning, everything so peaceful, so still as if the night and the snow had laid a silencing finger on life's dirge and stilled the song. You by the window, lost in thought, the falling snow had drawn a curtain around the house, around us – there was only us.

When you turned to hand me the tea tray, I was turned loose, once again and your playing, note after limpid note, sealed my fate.

Caitlin closed the journal, tears in her eyes. So in the end they had communicated, although it had been more his doing than hers. She wished she could tell him now that he had been right, that for the most part living was waiting to die, but how we spend that time, how we defend ourselves against despair, that is the trick – although she was still not sure that she was the right person to have taught it to him.

ㅁ

Work had become a narcotic, something that she craved in order to take the pain away: her daily routine, her patients, the latest crisis at the hospital, reading, researching, all this passed for life.

Dr. MacLean had called her in and gently probed her reaction to Philip's death. He had cited statistics of suicide rates for schizophrenics, for the hospital population in general, had reviewed with her that Philip had given no indication of being at risk; yes, it might have been prudent not to invite him home, such things were always unpredictable, but she needed to move on and consider this one of the risks inherent in their job. He also quoted something he had recently come across in his research – that the suicides of schizophrenics often amounted to the ultimate declaration of power and disdain on their part.

He had suggested talking might be helpful, but when she did, all that surfaced was guilt and self-doubt. A guilt that seemed there to stay and a self-doubt that could not be assuaged by working harder, giving more, reading more intensely than ever.

January had settled in like a deep freeze in her soul. It was colder than she ever remembered. The shiny, hard surface of the world seemed the perfect correlate to the profound cold that held her feelings in its grip.

Everything had become linked in her mind. Philip's death seemed to have become the catalyst for remembering all the other deaths in her life. Yet he, for all his lack of options, had chosen *when* to die, chosen *how* to die. All her losses: her parents, Nettie and Thomas, had been plucked out of rich, vibrant lives apparently filled with a limitless future, plucked out by the random hand of fate. The loss of Daniel, who insinuated himself at the tag end of these thoughts, had of course been more than anything her own doing.

Sometimes it seemed as if Philip's choice, and Philip himself, had crossed her path to teach her a lesson, or wake her up. Then again, she thought, perhaps this was just part of the mind's tendency to seek patterns, to search for meaning.

As part of her regimen to work in order to forget, she had followed through with her promise to Dr. Sparshott to spend one evening a week at College Heights Military Hospital, where she took down the case histories of the veterans that were part of the post-war trauma project. They had agreed on a format. He wanted a social history of each patient that would go well beyond the usual cursory history-taking. They aimed at a full picture of each person's pre-war functioning: their family and work, as well as a sense of their belief and value system whenever possible. It would act as a baseline from which to access the impact of the war experience.

At first, she had wondered how being female would affect what she would hear, whether it would be a hindrance rather than a help. However, she soon realized that it was an advantage. Her quiet receptivity seemed to make the veterans more willing to explain themselves. In talking to her, they could not assume any prior knowledge of their war experience and they did not need to fall back on the stoicism required by one male of the other. She was so clearly an outsider, someone who "did not know" that they could speak more freely, describe in more detail, open up into their own vulnerability and be soothed by her attentive and sympathetic listening.

Caitlin quickly found that taking a history invariably opened up present-day wounds. It was the *before* in relation to the *after* that constituted the fault line in their personality, the rift that needed to be healed. She also learned about her own body, finding that listening to people in pain, to revelations so filled with incomprehensible horror, not only left her feeling drained, but made her, in a strange way, one of the walking wounded.

Sometimes she suspected herself of wanting to douse pain with more pain. Listening to these personal narratives filled with losses of all kinds – the loss of idealism, the rupture with faith and goodness, the abandonment of reason, doubt in man's rational behaviour and the ever present danger of death – listening to all that, she felt she too was being drawn into a vast wheel of pain and a deeper knowledge of the world.

As if to save herself, she occasionally gave in to Syb's entreaties to join them for dinner, go to a concert or meet them at the harbour to watch the ice boating. A love of music was something both of them shared, and therefore she had finally agreed to be picked up for an evening concert at Massey Hall.

It helped, sitting next to Syb, who, as always, exuded vitality. Caitlin would not have believed how difficult it was to let the music affect her when her every feeling was armoured against the world. During the intermission she was grateful for Syb's light-hearted responses to everything and her amusing comments; they drew her away from the endless cycle of brooding self-contemplation. While walking up and down in the vestibule during the intermission, she was suddenly stopped by a hand on her arm and exclamations of "Caitlin, how nice!" It was Bella, on the arm of a sporty-looking young man. She responded to Caitlin's surprised look by laughing merrily, "You have not heard? Martin and I decided some time ago that things were not the same after his return. I am 'unengaged' once more! Let me introduce you to Gregory."

She had been listening to the young man in front of her reliving the horrors of the trenches for close to an hour and felt exhausted. As she put on her coat to meet the cab to take her home, she thought, "So much pain, so much damage."

Later, in the waning hours of the evening, she realized that her view of the world was changing, that nothing would ever hold the same innocence again. In one of those associative leaps that the mind seems prone to, she saw herself, suddenly at age seventeen, at the scene of what was later called "The Great Fire," on a cold day in April, 1904.

For some reason, memory provided her with images of great clarity. She was in her last year at the Bishop Strachan School for Girls; it was a few days after the Great Fire and it was finally considered safe to go and have a look at the devastation. For days, dense clouds of smoke had been seen south of College Heights and the air had been filled with the smell of charred wood and, apparently, gas. The heart of the wholesale district had been leveled. They had heard of the all-enveloping clouds of steam that were released as the firefighters tried to douse the white-hot mass of bricks, girders, and felled wooden telegraph poles. At night the whole sky had been lit up as if it were day. Pillaging had been reported, but also that firefighters had come from all over, from as far away as Peterborough and Buffalo, to do what they could do to help. It was an unheard-of event and the head mistress had decided that, once it was safe, they would go as a group to see for themselves.

In spite of all the rumours and first-person accounts, they were not prepared for what met their eye. Block after block of the centre of the city had met the same frightful ruin; it seemed as if not a single wall had been left intact, only the grid of the streets provided an anchoring point. As far as the eye could see, warehouse after warehouse, office building after office building, was reduced to a jagged, skeletal presence. A ghostly lack of life remained. It seemed as if the architectural monuments had been reduced to their original building blocks, as if one were returning to the earliest blueprint phase on the architect's drawing board. People, even their group of schoolgirls, tended to fall silent as the full impact of the scene revealed itself. She still remembered the unreality of it all, as if she were visiting a stage set, especially since, through the haze, you could still see unharmed chimney stacks, City Hall or the Customs House, depending on in which direction you looked. They, although intact, seemed as unreal as the rest, providing the finite boundaries of a glimpse into hell; and, she thought now, all that had been like a premonitory vision of what the Great War would soon have in store for them.

¤

Would she ever get used to the incessant noise, the dark clouds of smoke so typical for a workday in the city? She sympathized with the patients, who had no way of escaping them and who had to endure the endless clanging and shunting going on in the CNR yards, the noise coming from the Massey factory, the Smith Planing Mill and all the lesser wool mills and box manufacturers. There was no escape, especially since the Hospital's fresh air policy seemed to ensure that no noise was to be muffled by a closed window.

Sometimes when Caitlin felt the urge to escape the insularity of the Hospital, she would walk down Asylum Lane in the direction of the Hospital Farm where Asylum Creek wound its way southward. She remembered hearing that the original site had been known as Black Ash Swamp. However, wherever she turned, she could still see the Hospital itself with its imposing walls that regularly acted as a spur to patients to "go over the wall." As she continued her walk south, she could feel the industrial commercial power of the city pulsing all around her. It was with some relief that she returned to Queen Street, noting the beautiful YMCA building, the Gladstone Hotel nearby, and, of course, the library.

She had felt cold all day. Cold to the bone. She had tried warming her hands on the teapot, or putting them into her skirt pockets, but nothing seemed to touch the frozen part deep inside of her. The day had seemed endless and the trip home had been an unreal confabulation of sounds, penetrating smells and unsettling motion.

Mrs. Harris became concerned when Caitlin went straight to bed. She offered her herbal teas, warm water bottles and extra covers. Gratefully, Caitlin let herself be taken care of before she dropped off into the heavy, turgid depth of a troubled sleep. Dream fragments, bodily aches, damp, flushed skin, shaking chills, and finally fever, waxed and waned like the light behind the closed curtains of her bedroom.

All strength, all purpose, seemed to have seeped from her and left an aching shell of a body. She felt weaker and closer to nothingness than ever before. There seemed to be no need to open her eyes, or trace thought fragments to their logical conclusions; it seemed easier to just drift like that forever.

At times during her illness hallucinatory visions of white rippled south to the lake and to the north where they swept across granite wastes straight into Hudson Bay. She remembered feeling as if her future, written in invisible ink on this dreamscape, remained tantalizingly out of reach; yet she felt too weak to let it matter, it was more important to give in to sleep.

A cool, wet cloth stroked her face, defined her features to herself, ran up and down her arms lovingly, and cooled off her hands. Water splashed in a basin next to her as on the shores of her childhood, gentle strokes swept up her calves and legs and woke her up more fully. "Thank you" was all she could say, but it was a beginning.

Mrs. Harris's ministrations slowly took on definition. Her hands filling the decanter on her night table brought a cool glass to her lips, brushed her hair and rearranged her pillows. Yes, she had been quite ill. Her family doctor, Dr. Llewellyn, had been surprised at the virulence of her influenza and the way it seemed to have left her for a few worrisome days with no will to rally. He reminded Caitlin how invulnerable she had seemed two years ago, during the deadly influenza epidemic of 1918, in which, he added in his somewhat pedantic manner, more people had died than during the war.

Drifting through the timelessness of convalescence Caitlin kept hearing the disembodied line of one of Schubert's Lieder; "...and every sound, a sound of woe..." No accompanying melody, just this stark reminder of life's vulnerability. At times, just when she surfaced from a dreamless depth, this fragment would be her first conscious thought, like an uncomfortable "*memento mori.*" At other times, giving in to her general sense of lassitude, she would float in fragments of unsurpassed beauty, a meadow, for example, where every wildflower stood out with supernatural clarity, where she could smell freshly cut grass, or hear the eternal repetition of water coursing over stone. Surrounded by the warmth of a generous sun, she seemed immersed in an apotheosis of childhood itself.

Then just as suddenly, she would drift into a web of turbulent dreams and bereft mornings, where she would see herself running excitedly to share something with either her mother or her father, and then, nothing – a sudden stop, where loss could not be denied any longer. Once, she had woken up bathed in tears, torn from a dream, an all too real counterlife, with no clear memory of anything specific, only a desperate sense of abandonment and grief.

It seemed that, with her body laid low, her conscious will to fight undermined, she had finally submitted to letting the past affect her heart.

Recuperating meant resuming a schedule: going down for dinner, reading the *Globe*, catching up on her correspondence, and finally, wanting to be back at work. She had learned to accept some truth about her work while recuperating. She had admitted to herself how much her patients' plight preoccupied her on a day-to-day basis and how much her work refused to stay behind the hospital walls.

It seemed that Philip's death had started a process of remembering that, she felt instinctively, needed to be honoured. As Dr. Sparshott had put it when he came to visit her, "Your many losses want to be acknowledged, want to be grieved, Caitlin." And a bit later, "I'm not sure that taking these detailed case histories is the right thing for you at this time. Let's think about it when you feel better." When she did feel better, she knew that working with him on his project was important to her and needed to continue.

To Mrs. Harris's great surprise Caitlin had begun to reminisce with her about her parents. Caitlin, for her part, found that Mrs. Harris welcomed talking about the past and felt pleased to fill in any gaps for her. As a result, they had found themselves poring over the photograph album for hours at a time. Each photo seemed to trigger a flood of down-to-earth observations and anecdotes from Mrs. Harris. When they were finished she said, "I am so glad you finally asked about the past, Caitlin. When you were younger, you would not listen to any of this. Any mention of your parents and your face would set and one knew better than to pursue it."

Yes, she remembered. She also remembered how Nettie had tried to reminisce with her and she had met her with outright resistance. Caitlin had been polite, but intransigent. No tears, no complaints, just a silent armour-plating of the soul and a deep distrust of life's purposes.

In the weeks to come, Caitlin found that a renewed sense of hope had been sparked in her.

It was also during this time that she heard from Daniel. In his typically matter-of-fact manner he told her how he had received two promising job offers, one from a hospital in Boston, the other from Chicago. Either one would take him away from Canada for good. Apparently, both had merit and he was going to Chicago to find out more. He rambled on a bit more about how he sensed there were new areas opening up in psychology, perhaps in industry, for example, how to market consumer goods, or select people for certain kinds of jobs. Yes, he knew it sounded utopian at this point, but there was amazing potential, he believed. Caitlin had to smile to herself at this egocentric good-bye letter, but she realized once more that Daniel lived in a different world, one in which the future appeared untouched by recent history and the human miscry all around them.

In her spare time she found herself returning to Philip's notebook. After rereading his earlier notes and leafing through them, she found that he had started it from both ends and had worked towards the middle – as if towards a meeting of *two* minds. She found that it started with an anguished short poem:

I felt a cleavage in my mind
As if my brain had split;
I tried to match it, seam by seam,
But could not make them fit.

The thought behind I strove to join
Unto the thought before,
But sequence raveled out of reach
Like balls upon the floor.

Emily Dickinson, she realized. Her favourite poet. After that, several pages of notes, jottings or thought fragments chased each other across several pages. His handwriting, at times illegible, flew similarly across the lines, past margins and boundaries. Again, no dates or clues, that would allow her to place this condensation of suffering and pain into the proper context of her knowledge of him. The nursing staff had often commented on his long periods of lucidity that would suddenly vanish, as he appeared to turn inward, as if obeying a stark inner law. At those times, he had seemed to respond to some beautiful inner revelation, or a vision that held him spellbound. Often he had appeared literally frozen in the contemplation of an object as if it had suddenly disclosed to him the mysteries of existence. This watchful stare and tense posture, as if any movement could break the spell, she had recognized as part of the "aura" that often initiated a psychotic break, which was frequently followed by more overt delusions. Philip's usual quiet and unassuming manner had been known to stiffen at those times into haughtiness. An impatient, imperious tone would creep into his speech and restless pacing and low-key mumbling would precede his less and less coherent utterances.

Turning to the first page of this "backlog," she read:

"..........*today, He finally spoke, loud and clear, bright as searchlight, a flare, just illuminating my spot. He wants me to stop this madness… finally my waiting is paying off … the others will never know, only I am chosen.*

The Huns, He says, need to be stopped, not just 'over there', but here, here above all… He says I can will it, can do it by plugging into His god-like power. I did it once before, last winter, when it was getting dark outside… I willed the war to stop ———— ***and it did.*** *All the church bells rang, the factories blew their whistles, the streetcars and motorcars blew their horns… the people had a parade, a victory parade… and He was pleased, and I knew, I alone had done it…."*

Here his thought processes were interrupted by tight pencil cross-hatchings that suggested a fine grid. Boxes packed within boxes and lines receding off the page.

Further on:

I feel the sucking of the mud at my boots and I can see a faint brown stain gain in intensity, I can make out the horses and the riders, column after column of ghost horses and ghost riders pass in front of my eyes. Their strained eyeballs fixed in a kind of premature rigor mortis.

… their swollen carcasses discarded by the wayside, just like the useless guns that have fallen from the hands of the men, who lie scattered everywhere.

I try to look through my lens which makes everything look like a stage set, or sometimes, like a painting, but I cannot, will not, do it anymore…

The curtain is torn; I can see a glimpse of the stage. It is empty. There are no actors, there is no play, there is no make-believe. EVERYONE HAS GONE HOME.

And so it went, more or less comprehensible, more or less detached from our notions of what is real, what is fantasy, what is madness. As if such categories could be reified. Caitlin felt a great sadness at seeing the two sides of Philip, back to back so to speak, engaged in a headlong rush towards a meeting that he had circumvented by his decision that night, at the stairwell.

She held his notebook in her hands and thought, "I am still listening, Philip…"

There were days when the last few months with their heavy burden seemed to slide off her. She mentally compared herself to a snake shedding its skin, leaving the protective armour behind which in its delicate transparency was still true to her former self, while a new, vulnerable and raw self eased itself into the world.

Her progress was halting and cautious initially, but then new energies gathered, and she found herself making changes: changes to the house, her bed-sitting room needed to be more of a study, the dark curtains would have to make way for soft pastels, the walls were to be lightened and the garden seemed to require a small pond, water lilies, frogs. Even her work needed to be rethought. How happy was she with it, really? How much was she allowed to stretch her wings in that setting? How did she want to spend the rest of her life? How important was loving and being loved? And what made her believe that one needed to wait until love found one? No end to questions that seemed to spawn new ones as quickly as she thought of them.

She had often wondered about how to describe the gap she sensed between the experience of the moment and later insights that arrived only when the same moment was recollected in tranquility. How often had she found that, in the moment itself, all she did was react automatically, suspending her judgement? Things had a way of unrolling, inevitably, smoothly, according to the social script set in motion on the first day of her life; while at a deeper level, another part of her seemed to *know* more. Sometimes, if she stayed receptive enough, that knowledge would surface as insight. Caitlin hoped the moment would come when she would act wisely *in* the moment.

The day was unseasonably cold. Hopefully, it was winter's last stand before it passed into spring. Caitlin half-ran into the building and up the stairs, partly to escape the frigid wind and partly because she worried about being late. At the top of the staircase she looked up and thought she recognized Martin Rhys in the male figure disappearing down the shadowy hallway. She knew that was possible, since Martin was one of Dr. Sparshott's patients. Strange to think that every Wednesday when she had come to work here, he might have been leaving. Mentally, she saw two strangers, "intimate strangers," one ascending the stairs and the other descending.

¤

A measured prolonged sound seemed to have invaded her sleep, her slow waking up. Her eyes closed against the light that she sensed outside, Caitlin found herself anxiously anticipating the next soft sound. Drifting towards recognition, she realized that what she heard was water dripping off the roof.

It was easy to get up after that. She drew back the drapes, pushed up the inside windowpane and released the small oval wooden shutter on the storm window that opened up three perfectly round holes to the world. A fresh breeze grazed her hands and lifted the lace curtains. Outside, the influx of warmer air was beginning to change the wintry hues of the garden and the sky itself. Everywhere, she could hear the tender drip of ice being released.

Finally, always just when she was ready to despair at living in this unforgiving climate, the white shroud would lift off the landscape and life reasserted itself.

Dr. Sparshott, Joshua, was in a hurry as usual, but she knew she was a serious item on his agenda when he sat down in front of her, stretched out his long legs and leaned back in his chair in the closest approximation of relaxation she had seen him assume.

He wanted to discuss her 'interim report' that summarized her interviews with the veterans. He commented warmly on its lucidity, organization and especially on her level of insight. He seemed excited about the links he sensed between her histories and any treatment outcomes he had seen so far, provisional though all conclusions were at this point. Often so removed, Joshua could become animated by ideas and, given resonance, could take off on flights of inspired speculation.

Caitlin listened attentively to his vision of where this research might lead. As he continued to expound his ideas, she realized that he was leading up to asking her to join him in the continued exploration of war-induced trauma and, perhaps, the after-effects of trauma in general. "Caitlin, you know that at the Hospital you will never get a chance to do any meaningful work under your own name. You know the rigid hierarchy there and the difficulties of being accepted...I do; that is why I left; and you as a woman..."

She knew he was right, knew it especially after the response to the manuscript of her article, tentatively entitled, "Attempts at a Talking Cure with Schizophrenic Patients." It had become clear that her voice would be muted, hidden behind anonymous initials if she was lucky and the article ever saw print. She also knew that in all her time there, she had not met with this kind of excitement about the "new," the as yet to be discovered, and she knew most of all, that something in her moved in response to the idea of discovery itself, to working together, being an equal partner, learning from each other. While she let him talk on to convince her, she knew deep inside that the dice had been rolled already and there could only be one answer.

As Caitlin walked home she found herself musing on how tiny, insignificant-seeming steps could lead ultimately to the big changes and turnabouts in one's life. There seemed to be no one moment of deliberate decision-making, only moments when a series of almost carelessly made choices culminated in giving a completely new twist to a life. Today, with spring unfolding all around her, with new doors opening up in her professional life, she felt that she might finally be ready to bury her dead. And she wondered whether Joshua had meant something like that when he had said, "You are perfect for the job. You not only know about loss, but you seem to have moved beyond it."

She had not really answered that, but had left saying, "You know that I will think seriously about what you have said; your offer deserves nothing less." Think she would, but only as part of a lifetime reflex. The decision to join his program had sprung up fully-formed in her heart while he had talked.

Dr. MacLean, when he heard her news, had smiled paternally and joked about her making her getaway from the "old boys' club." Then more seriously, he said, "Caitlin, you know I wish you well. I am sure you have not made this decision lightly. As a matter of fact, your serious commitment to anything you have ever undertaken has been very much appreciated around here, and, yes, another professional setting might be more receptive to what you have to offer." They had left on good terms, Dr. MacLean finishing off with his favourite, "Your father would have been proud of you." His ultimate seal of approval.

And there, in a nutshell, was the problem.

Once having made her decision, she could not help feeling wistful as she walked in and out of the still imposing institution for the next few weeks. She felt she owed it a lot of learning, and she knew that she had let all of its concerns, routines and, above all, its patients become very much a part of her life. A life aside, a life separated by walls of brick and prejudice that for her had become more permeable through her own involvement and eagerness to know it.

As she left today, the weather brought one more surprise. Although the Hospital boasted huge windows everywhere, her concentration and the intensity of her work had been such that, come evening, she found herself startled by a storm raging outside. A veritable blizzard – in April! All vision was obliterated. The storm must have been gathering for a while. She decided to call a cab rather than sit freezing in a stalled streetcar, possibly having to make her way home on foot. Having decided to wait in the relative warmth of the vestibule, she stood by the glass door, where she could feel the clean, sharp cold from the glass pane reaching her face and observe the snowflakes turning into soft, elliptical runnels of water in front of her eyes. Timeless space opened up in front of her, inviting the new – all she needed to do was wait.

Acknowledgements

I gratefully acknowledge Luciano Iacobelli's insightful reading of my text and his editorial guidance, as well the meticulous reading of copy editor, Allan Briesmaster. Our work together has been fruitful and inspiring.

I would also like to remember John Court of the *Archives for the History of Canadian Psychiatry and Mental Health Services* (Centre for Addiction and Mental Health) for his enthusiastic help while I was doing my research and for facilitating the inclusion of my work in the *Research in Progress Seminar.*

Other Quattro Novellas